TRISTANO

Tristano

A Novel

NANNI BALESTRINI

Translated by Mike Harakis
With a Foreword by Umberto Eco

VERSO
London • New York

This English-language edition first published by Verso 2014
Translation © Mike Harakis 2014
First published as *Tristano*
© DeriveApprodi 2007

1 3 5 7 9 10 8 6 4 2

Verso
UK: 6 Meard Street, London W1F 0EG
US: 20 Jay Street, Suite 1010, Brooklyn, NY 11201
www.versobooks.com

Verso is the imprint of New Left Books

ISBN-13: 978-1-78168-169-5

British Library Cataloguing in Publication Data
A catalogue record for this book is available from the British Library

Library of Congress Cataloging-in-Publication Data
A catalog record for this book is available from the Library of Congress

Typeset in Fournier by MJ & N Gavan, Truro, Cornwall
Printed in Italy by Associazione Padre Monti – Saronno (VA) – Italy

Foreword

What Is Balestrini Up to Now?

Umberto Eco

Pascal used to say: 'Let nobody say that I've said nothing new. The layout of the subject is new. When playing tennis both players use the same ball, but one hits it better than the other.'

Pascal said, 'Let no one say that I have said nothing new; the arrangement of the material is new. When we play tennis, we both play with the same ball, but one of us places it better.'

The above is not a way of finding excuses for a lack of originality, but of affirming that originality and creativity are nothing more than the chance handling of a combination. That is, that the creative genius is capable of combining – with greater rapidity, more critical sense of what should be discarded, greater intuition in the choice of what should be saved – the same material that had been made available to the failed genius.

If, to some, the proposal seems limitative, just think about the alphabet: it is a kit of ready-to-use elements (of variable number depending on the language, ranging from twenty to thirty) that the good Lord, nature or chance made available to Dante (who composed the *Divine Comedy* with it), to Hitler (who composed *Mein Kampf* with it) and to Calvino's obscure brigadier, who composed a pathetic official report with it.

The dream of infinite combinations has obsessed many people. If this were not a simple introduction, we could start from Cabbalistic combination, Raymond Lull's wheels, or

Giordano Bruno; but since I started with Pascal, I would like to mention some combinatorial fantasies that were circulating in his time.

In the seventeenth century, G. P. Harsdörffer (*Mathematische und philosophische Erquickstunden*, 1651) proposed a game where 264 units (prefixes, suffixes, letters, and syllables) were disposed on five wheels to generate 97,209,600 German words, including inexistent ones, which could be used for creative-poetic purposes. But if this could be done for German, why not conceive a machine capable of generating all possible languages?

In his commentary *In Spherum Ioannis de Sacro Bosco* (1607), Christopher Clavius considered how many *dictiones*, that is, how many terms could be produced with the twenty-three letters of the alphabet (at the time there was no distinction between 'u' and 'v'), combining them two by two, three by three and so on, up to considering twenty-three-letter words. He provided the various mathematical formulae for this calculation, and he stopped at a certain point in front of the immensity of the possible results – especially when repetitions were taken into consideration.

In 1622, Pierre Guldin wrote a *Problema arithmeticum de rerum combinationibus* in which he calculated all the enunciations that could be generated with twenty-three letters, independently of whether they made sense or could be pronounced, but without calculating the repetitions, and he found that the number of words – of variable length from two to twenty-three letters – was more than seventy thousand billion billion (to write them out would require more than a million billion billion letters). To be able to imagine this number one should imagine writing all these words in 1,000-page notebooks, each with 100 lines per page and sixty characters per line: one would need 257 million billion of such notebooks. And if they were placed in a library – of which Guldin studied the disposition separately, the size, the circulating conditions – if cube-shaped buildings of 432 feet per side were available, each capable of housing 32 million volumes, then 8,052,122,350 such libraries would be needed. But what kingdom could contain so many buildings? Given the entire surface available on the planet, we could house only 7,575,213,799!

In 1636, Father Marin Mersenne, in his *Harmonie universelle*, posed the same problem by taking into consideration, besides the *dictiones*, the '*canti*' (or musical sequences) that could be generated. Mersenne touched upon the problem of a universal language capable of potentially containing all possible languages, but with a great sense of moderation proposed to generate only pronounceable words. Even within this limit, he perceived the shiver of infinity. The same was true of the *canti* that can be generated on an extension of three octaves, and so twenty-two notes, without repetitions (the first glimmer of what would become the dodecaphonic series!). Mersenne observed that to write down all these *canti* one would need more reams of paper than those necessary to fill the distance between heaven and earth, even if each sheet were to contain 720 *canti* each with twenty-two notes, and every ream were compressed so much that it was less than an inch thick: because the number of *canti* that could be generated with twenty-two notes would be 1,124,000,727,777,607,680,000, and, dividing them by the 362,880 chants that can be contained in a ream, one would obtain in any case a sixteen-figure number – while only 28,826,640,000,000 inches separate the centre of the earth from the stars. And if one were to write down all these *canti*, at the rate of 1,000 per day, it would take 22,608,896,103 years and twelve days.

Leibniz, in a few pages entitled *De l'horizon de la docrine humaine*, posed the problem that had already fascinated Mersenne: what is the highest number of enunciations, true or false and even meaningless, that can be formulated using a fixed, finite alphabet of twenty-four letters? The problem is keeping to enunciable truths, and to enunciations that can be written down. Given twenty-four letters, one can form thirty-one-letter words (of which Leibniz finds examples in Greek and in Latin), and with the alphabet it is possible to produce 24^{32} thirty-one-letter words. But how long can an enunciation be? Since it is also possible to imagine enunciates as long as books, the sum of the enunciates, true or false, that a man can read in the course of his life – calculating that he reads 100 sheets a day and that each sheet contains 1,000 letters – is 3,650,000,000. But let us presume this man lived a thousand years, seeing that, according to legend, this happened to the alchemist Artephius. 'The greatest period we can enunciate, or the largest book that a man can read, will come to 3,650,000,000 [letters], and the number of all the truths, falsehoods or periods that can be enunciated, or rather are readable, pronounceable or unpronounceable, meaningful or not, will come to $\frac{24^{3650000000001} - 24}{23}$ [letters].'

But if we were to take an even larger number – let's consider the possibility of using 100 letters of the alphabet – then we would have a number of letters expressible in *1* followed by 7,300,000,000,000 zeros, and we would need a thousand scriveners to work for approximately thirty-seven years.

The Leibnizian argument, in this case, is that – even considering such an astronomical number of enunciates (and if we wanted we could keep increasing the number *ad libitum*) – they could not be thought of and understood by humanity, and in any case they would exceed the number of true and false enunciates that humanity is capable of producing and understanding. Therefore, paradoxically, the number of enunciates that can be formulated would still only be finite, and there would come a time when humanity would start reproducing the same enunciates again, which allows Leibniz to touch upon the theme of apocatastasis, that is, a universal reintegration (we might call it an eternal return).

Here the vertigo of Borges's 'Library of Babel' (not to mention Mallarmé's *Livre* or the *Hundred Thousand Billion Poems* by Queneau) were being anticipated, and *ad abundantiam*: where not only does the consciousness of the infinite productivity of language appear, but also the belief that (as I said at the beginning) there are potentially contained, in a very limited series of letters and sounds, not only all the literary texts that have been produced by man, from Hesiod to Joyce, and all the musical sequences ever heard until now, from Pythagoras to Luciano Berio, but also all the texts and compositions that will be produced in the next 100 million years (if the earth does not destroy itself before then).

Just as all future scientific discoveries should in some way be contained in the algorithms that govern natural events, so all artistic creations should potentially already be contained in the fundamental elements, sounds, letters, intervals, shades, lines, geometrical figures available to our species. The creative man will not, then, be he who has deduced something new *ex nihilo*, but he who has identified it, by intuition, by trial and error, by chance – or by that infinite patience which for Flaubert was a sign of genius – amid the gangue that enclosed it and concealed it from our eyes.

However, in quoting writers like Mallarmé and Queneau we have passed from the combination of 'linguistic atoms' that lack meaning (letters of the alphabet or sounds) to the combination of textual portions, real 'excerpts' already furnished with a sense of their own, and which it should nevertheless be possible to combine without giving the impression of a random jumble.

Breaking Manzoni's novel *The Betrothed* into sequences of ten lines (or even into blocks as long as chapters) and freely recombining these segments, one would not obtain much of anything (it would be embarrassing to let Don Rodrigo die before he becomes infatuated with Lucia); but with more open texts (for example *Finnegans Wake*) some interesting results could be obtained. A few pieces might not fit together well, but our old pioneers of combinatory theory had already considered the problem of whether to combine unpronounceable words as well, like an Italian word with five consonants in a row. An alphabet does not have rules, but a language does. Even Dante, using the Italian alphabet, could not compose any sequence which was mathematically possible, but only those permitted by the vocabulary and syntax of the Italian language.

If we wanted to arrange the pieces of an infinitely variable story, it would be better for the textual blocks to be 'prepared', like pieces of Lego, each already designed to fit together with other pieces in multiple ways. Such is the case with Balestrini's book, whose game is 'regulated' in the sense that it does not aim to celebrate fortuity so much as the possibility of an elevated number of possible outcomes. Programmers say that with Balestrini's project it is possible to compose 109,027,350,432,000 different books.

Balestrini is not new to combinatory games, which go back to his infancy as a writer. But at one time these billions of different tales might have aspired only to a theoretical, or, in current parlance, virtual, existence. Whereas today, thanks not only to computers that can quickly combine in the most vertiginous ways, but also to digital printing and printing on demand, the reader can have 'in flesh and blood' either a different copy of the tale from all the others (which represents both the triumph and the death of the numbered edition, seeing that each copy would be number 1), or any number of them, for purposes of comparison (time permitting).

I see three possibilities for the potential readers of this book: (1) to acquire a single copy and read it as a unique, unrepeatable and unchangeable text; (2) to acquire many copies and have fun following the unexpected outcomes of the combination; (3) to choose just one of the many texts available, considering it to be the best – just as some say that God, out of all the worlds he could have created, chose the existing one as the best of all possible worlds (I would hate to think of the others). In the end, it is what all great writers have done when wrestling with the vertigo granted by the alphabet: they could compose infinite texts (and maybe they have made infinite attempts, throwing more pages in the bin than those which are finally bound in a volume), but they ultimately settled on one. And only by doing the same will Balestrini's readers have become co-authors (or maybe the sole authors): by exercising their own creativity.

Certainly the game requires time, as we have seen. But can we waste time posing the problem of time, when combinatory theory promises us eternity?

Note on the Text

Nanni Balestrini

In 1961, I created *Tape Mark I*, a poetic experiment made possible by using the combining possibilities of an IBM calculator (which was the name given to computers back then). A series of pieces of sentences were put together one after the other, until they formed sequences of verses, following simple rules transformed into algorithms which guided the machine. The number of possible results was huge, and just a small number of variants were published in the *Almanacco Bompiani 1962*.

At the time, this experiment was very controversial: it had never been done before, and the press in Italy and abroad fantasised about the effects of producing these machine-made poems. In reality it was only a case of taking advantage of a new instrument capable of creating many combinations very rapidly, thereby introducing an element of randomness.

Using the same instrument, I then decided to create a novel. Compared to the poetic experiment, this one had the advantage of having a physical product as a result, a book, which could be reproduced a number of times (theoretically unlimited) – yet each one being very different, as a result of the different combinations of verbal elements that the calculator would obtain each time using the predetermined programme. But the printing technologies of the time did not permit the realisation of such a project. Therefore in 1966 I was only given the possibility of printing one version of it, with the Feltrinelli publishing house, called *Tristano* – an ironic homage to the archetype of the love story. The book aroused a lot of interest from critics for its experimental and provocative aspect, which made one reconsider the notions of characters and plot, time and space. A careful interpretation of the text (which obviously doesn't take into consideration the combinatorial aspect of the current edition) can be found in Jacqueline Risset's foreword to the French translation, published in 1972 by Éditions du Seuil.

Today, forty years later, the evolution of digital printing makes it possible to realise the old project, and Xerox machines are capable of printing dissimilar books very quickly. The present publication of *Tristano* (not republished since 1966) could therefore be faithful to its intended form: an edition of unique, numbered copies, each containing a different combination of the same verbal material, elaborated by the original calculator's programme.

This operation puts the single format and predefined dogma of the original version into crisis: it was a literary work dictated by the stiff determinism of Gutenbergian mechanical typography, which produces only identical examples. The fact that the mechanical reproduction process can be surpassed by that offered by digital technologies seems to hint at the infinite variety of shapes in nature, where each element, from the leaf of a tree to a human being, is always a slightly different variant of a non-existing prototype. Likewise, a spoken story changes more or less when told to different listeners, or at a different time. And in this way a literary work, a novel, can be created, thanks to new technologies, no longer as an immutable unicum, but in a series of equivalent variants, each materialized in a book, the copy and personal story of each reader.

This is only the first experiment that exploits in a limited way the great potential offered by technological innovation, thanks to which it becomes possible to represent effectively the complexities and unpredictability of contemporary reality, of our day-to-day life. And to experiment with a new way of conceiving literature, and novels in particular, offering original possibilities for freedom of creation and communication with the audience.

Chapter One

Thank you for letting me sleep. There were some flowers in a vase and a long sofa in front of the fireplace. I hate all the others and I hope they'll all die women and children young and old. Yes real pity. Nobody has pity on me or wants to help me. She kept on yawning. I stopped the car in front of a house and got out. I came back on the 46 and spent the afternoon fishing in the lake but without that much enthusiasm. The house was about seven kilometres away. I slowed down gradually on entering the built-up area. He lowered the window even more and rested his hand on it. The horizon to the north is clear at sunset. He always told me I shouldn't think. He started running. I don't have a headache anymore. Stop wasting your time with your lovely little fantasies. Her hair framed her face with two soft waves that reached her shoulders.

I continue to walk always treading on the outside part of my foot. The same subjects in a state of wakefulness constantly responded with a normal inflection. The aforementioned researchers in repeated experiments carried out on patients who were made to regress to the first month of their lives. I saw a trickle of water dribble out from under the bathroom door. I saw the leaves move slowly. A small cape of the same colour fell over her shoulders. Standing struggling to keep his balance he laughs. As is well known this reflex is characterised in newborn babies by a dorsal extension of the big toe while in more mature individuals it is marked by a plantar flexion. The mortality of the elderly reaches very high peaks. I saw C race past in a taxi. At the end of the street the lights were going on and off.

The amnesty sealed the failure of the purge and it was the key disposition to wipe the slate clean of Fascist responsibility. The man in the street can get out of his responsibilities by simply claiming that the matter does not concern him. It is the fence that delimits and assures what has been censured. It is the well of a history of which you want to lose the course and memory. And what is the relationship between identity and struggle. But let's get back to the husband. C hadn't let him come in. What would you do. I don't think I can start again like I did before. I know myself well enough. The only thing to do. You could at least close the door. He walks toward the door. I can't do it. Doors that open and close letting in air and extracting it through sudden breaks barriers gaps and outlets. He decided to do neither of the two things. A strong wind was blowing. C shivered under the sheets.

He asked me to get someone to lend me some money. Other things are always talked about. I'm willing to do anything to help him. He was not all that interested in what she was saying. The sky is pale toward the east before the rising of the sun whose rays are refracted in an area of white clouds rising in strata or tufts that increase forming dense dark masses. We can go out now if you want. She lets go of the shutter suddenly went back into the room and lay down on the bed. Because I love my husband. The fear that I too would judge her without indulgence fuelled that nervousness that immediately exploded in the confession that follows. The lack of affection. She said she had gone for a walk along the shore of the lake. Three thick cables clearly spaced penetrated into the dock dropping from a pole and supported by two others they went back toward the house on the opposite side of the road.

I can't remember anything anymore. I don't want to talk about it. The sky has never been so grey. He wondered whether his life really had any meaning. It is difficult to admit we are not coherent with ourselves in every aspect of our personality. C looked at himself in the mirror trying to remember what his appearance was like the first time they had met. We are rather a mosaic of character traits which often clash with one another as a result of the different experiences undergone. A painfully ambiguous mirror effect. He put out his cigarette. I answered that things would probably change. C said that he felt like going out going all the way down to the lake to see the boats go by. Variable cloudiness with scattered thunderstorms. In this way showing that you don't speak or remain silent you don't enter or exit the house but you live in an inbetween state in which it is possible not to make practical decisions and be serenely irresponsible.

A cat runs from one row of parked cars to the one in which I find myself. I turned the car and pulled up. On reaching the bank of the lake he wondered whether it was worth it. A long time had gone by. He had the impression he was wasting his time. The street seemed totally deserted. I didn't know the street very well. Mean streets. A person who is scared above all of herself. Treat life as if it were a game. Life consists first and foremost in the fact that a human being in every instant is himself and also another. I find that very difficult to picture. Silence had fallen in the room. C seemed to take it as a personal insult. It's written in the book he protested. I'm being serious and I believe this may be a good starting point. The following page contains more detailed information. I'm not C. I am the book. We talked all night. I want to go to sleep I don't want to argue with you.

The scene was completely deserted. Wherever she looked black clouds heavy with rain filled the sky up to the line of the horizon. Let's continue. Let's talk about it. I'm having trouble following you. What's there to tell. Other pictures overlap without any specific order some are out of focus and nearly unrecognisable. C's profile in the mirror as she combs her hair. The red sun on the horizon amongst the dark clouds. Her slender legs sticking out from under the sheets. Yellow and red flowers on the side of the road. Running along the windswept beach. Big smiling eyes. The rubble of a bombed-out building. The chocolate grinder. The cave immersed in darkness. The red cylinder that rotates extremely rapidly. The white house on top of the hill. The aeroplane coming in to land. C in her pistachio-coloured dress. The lake surrounded by pine trees. You can't go back said C.

Blood beats in her temples her hands tremble and her eyes glaze over. I wake up suddenly in the armchair because the telephone rings. Water enters the metal pipe under ordinary pressure which then comes out of the holes in the form of a myriad of jets that spurt onto the walls of the cylinders. He put it back down and the glass tinkled on the polished tabletop. An intonation of various hues of yellow that made the place warm and inviting. The sun high on the horizon and entirely or partially hidden by the clouds through which the rays filter in a characteristic way. Her hair between her lips. She rolls over leaning on her elbow and turned her face toward him. What am I going to do with it. He holds her tight by the waist and shoulder stroking her long red hair then went back and sat down on the edge of the bed. He moved downwards his head fell back onto the pillow.

The big toe on my right foot hurts and so I try and walk on the outside of my foot. She pulled the sheet up to her chin hung up reached out and caressed his cheek. Nobody can help me. Here she went to the bathroom. The whistle which has the objective of sonorizing the powder works on low-pressure compressed air. The others are on full blast. They are all on full. The particles are enlarged by agglutination and they attach on the walls of the cylinder from which they are taken up by a thin film of water. I was only ten years old when the war ended and so I didn't realise that the war had finished I didn't even realise that there had been this damn war and so I missed the great experience of the Liberation. That flows like fresh water leaving the unsolved problems that are absolutely refractory to the impellent necessities of breaking the mould shown by a society and a culture suffering from traditionalism.

The hand loosens its grip. Her normally low and husky voice trembled a little. The device is based on ultrasound and is composed of a metallic cylinder at one end of which is placed a whistle generator of ultrasounds that are reflected to the other end of the cylinder with an adjustable cap. Her hands held his body and she raised her hands to his face and she brushes against it. He came out of the bathroom she clenched her fists and got in the shower. She fell back onto the pillow and lay there gazing up at the ceiling. He empties the glass and puts it on the bedside table. She moves slowly under his body. The gravel path flanks the new residential holiday village and goes into the woods. The tundra interspersed with little clumps of arboreal vegetation dominates this region. The plants wither as if they were affected by consumption. They walked together on the pavement where the sun was not shining until the end of the street. He walked on the grass between the trees.

Don't be angry with me she said in a whisper. We 'll stay and look for another thirty seconds then we 'll leave. C asked me to stay that night too. Don't switch off the light. Anyway said C don't you think that one is master to do what he wants with his own life. The sound of his voice shook me from my state of half-sleep. All right all right but now that's enough of this story. Let's get out of here let's go and get a bit of fresh air. They had slept until midday and had gone to the beach after lunch. When he went out a few minutes later he had a lean composed face. What's wrong didn't you have a good time. Forget about that story let's go and get a coffee somewhere. He screwed up his eyes looking at the horizon veiled in mist. Think twice before doing it. The question is not so much the story itself but rather what effects it might produce what developments it might have what dynamics it might set in motion.

She has her blonde hair pulled back by a silver clip tanned skin from her life by the seaside luminous teeth. C was her best friend. The gold bracelets that tinkled on her wrist were one of his presents. She remembered the first time they had gone to C. What made you think of that. C stopped turning to him with a puzzled look on her face. What are you afraid of. Of abandoning yourself to your feelings. Do I really need to say the same thing over and over again. She couldn't finish the sentence. I've got nothing else to say. It is the moment in which you realise that language offers no guarantee at all. It's the unconditional loss of language that starts. When your feelings can't be expressed. Some things are done recklessly. I didn't know how to answer. A strange feeling. As if I couldn't breathe. I don't know how to explain it. Let's go and get something to eat now.

I'd like something to drink. The street that led out of town went toward the sea. Pines are accompanied by holly oaks and downy oaks while the undergrowth is characterised by mastics cistuses Mediterranean buckthorns strawberry trees and malus sylvestris. Cut short at every turn by an unexpected deviation. It had been anticipated that this would happen. That's how it is in the book. Why asked C thrusting his hand forward. To discover a real aspect of reality. He pulled her closer without meeting any resistance. He had not had the time to understand what was happening. C smiled with an innocent air without answering. You still haven't drunk enough. The next day he telephoned C to find out what his reaction was. He tried in vain to reconstruct the whole story. I carried on reading carefully. Many sentences recur. They were all names I didn't know. It depends on the point of view which changes every time C tried to reassure her.

Then trams buses and private vehicles started to stop repeatedly from the outskirts toward the centre in Piazzale del Cimitero Monumentale in Foro Buonaparte in Piazza Fontana along Cerchia dei Navigli. To this end the research carried out by Gildo Frank Bowers Buch True and Stephenson on the plantar reflex of the big toe is particularly interesting. She said that she needed a change of scene. I often got him to lend me money. She lets herself fall back toward him. Then she raises the packet a little and offers it to C who shakes his head. He smiled weakly. She glared at him as if it were of little importance. They suddenly look each other in the eyes. Still smiling C nodded her head. Take the tree-lined avenue until you reach the vicinity of the lake. She stopped again stubbed out the cigarette she had just lit and finished the tea that was left in the cup.

He had a voice of level pitch monotone and relaxing. Nothing had changed. And I was wondering how he had the audacity to talk about the resistance and not feel sick when talking about the present. And as we are ten years younger and haven't had to live through the tough war years we can't accept these cop-outs. The spirit of insistence should have become the basis of the Republic but you have failed and are failing in this. He went over to the window without speaking. Some figures appeared on the screen which were immediately taken down by those present. He looked for his glass and took another draught. A few drops of sweat beaded his tanned face. Why are you pulling my hair. On awakening a few hours later he saw C in the same position. Thingy has started a new narration.

The street is completely deserted and all the windows are closed. If you are very lucky you might even see a bear but you're more likely to come across a few shy lost hedgehogs. You take the not very appealing path but after about a hundred metres the road improves and you can continue without any problems along the noisy foamy river thick with willows. They had gone down to the C hotel at about midday they had been on a long walk. You need to go back to C and proceed down the 46 for a couple of kilometres until you come to an abandoned sawmill. From here the narration proceeds more quickly and confidently. We start looking everywhere in vain until C had the idea of leaving. Looking around without seeing him. A pole without roots planted in the ground and not even being planted deep enough.

Pause. A gust of wind can blow it over and when it falls on the ground it falls with a great thud because there is nothing absolutely nothing that can hold it up. She sits. I'd like you to kill me because I'll never have the courage to do it myself. The two indices flank each other rapidly and remain stuck together for a moment. One leg was stretched out and open you feel C's hands in your hair. C bursts into tears. His painful right foot. They go off in opposite directions. It's easy to miss it so you should keep your eye on the right-hand side of the road. And where shall we go now. The main danger is in very foggy winter days or when there is a low blanket of cloud over the town. The weather is overly clear so that objects that are as a rule invisible can be made out distinctly or magnified due to the phenomenon of refraction.

He was looking for another story to tell. He goes and tells all about what he's got in his drawers. She fights it by continually creating new verbal situations. He looked up at me quickly and looked away again. He's always got new things to add. And now we need to start again. Follow another silence. The situation was becoming particularly serious in Piazzale XXIV Maggio and at Porta Ticinese. I asked to talk to C. A debate about whether C's identity should be revealed follows. A strong smell of smoke hung in the room. Still leaning on the table as if he were sleeping. A woman's voice answered me. Yes. She turns other pages still yawning. From that point it extends along the circle of the ramparts and quickly reaches the nearby junctions. Bronchial diseases and pulmonary emphysemas increase in a short time.

He walked slowly on the sun-streaked pavement. Later he was putting his hands in freezing cold water after having whispered a word. Two new names were given and a third is easily recognisable. Round the corner the sun shone in your eyes and the air was warmer. A long thin rivulet of water slowly advances on the asphalt afterward this word was sufficient to cause a contraction of the arteries. Atrocious terrible solitude. As if it were the photograph of a horizontal tree. It was no longer a simple hand rail but a metal cable charged with electricity that arrived as far as the platform. After C had joined her he started getting undressed. At first the subject put his hands in freezing cold water and the arteries contracted. I feel so unhappy and I really want to die.

He would arrive before nightfall without any problem even though the light was already fading. I'm happy you arrived before the others. By giving the obstacle different shapes you will in general produce a variation of the possibilities of bypassing and at the same time you might be able to grade the difficulty the situation presents. She paused. A word like any other. She puts down the cup and lights a cigarette. It was a long time before I met you. He looked toward the window where C had been. You've been crying. She was by the fire in front of everyone a little way off C was looking out of a window. He crossed the hall again climbed the stairs and went back into his room. She waits still like that for about three minutes perhaps more quivering a little. I think you want to talk about C. I think that's enough. What have you done. I was broke once and I went to see her.

Chapter Two

He set their two glasses down on the coffee table and took her hands in his and got her to stand up. He felt her hand on his shoulders. Her hair framed her face with two soft waves that reached her shoulders. She kept on yawning. Okay said C. She takes a book and C catches up with her. We kneel in the middle of the room with our elbows on the floor. He brushed her cheek with his lips then he kissed her mouth. While I turn my back on her and dial the number on the telephone she gets undressed piling her clothes on a chair then she lies down on the bed under the sheet her head held tight between her elbows. She had only filled the bottom two rows and he was already placing the books in the middle of the shelf. Her eyes were closed and her breathing was laboured. The temperature had dropped noticeably during the night. I've got an idea.

After periods of eruptions drops of hard calcareous water from the mountain streams filter down through the rocks and gradually leave transparent strata on the walls or form columns of stalactites or stalagmites that hang from the vault or rise from the floor until they meet. Jesting. Besides the rivers rarely flow parallel to a coast or parallel to each other for any distance roads however often follow the coast and it is not infrequent that they run parallel to each other. Changing the subject for the first time. And then you met C. I asked to talk to C. The third name is not complete. And when he had reached the peak of his career it was inevitable that he would feel more and more dispossessed and excluded. That was why I feared him. The last class consists of fleeting indices of a movement. When did you first meet. And did you have intimate relationships with him. Only once. In the end he realised it was unbearable.

There the river looks like a rivulet and the trees go down all the way to the bank. She hangs up before I can even say ciao. Who attract each other with their minds to physically run away like crazy finding themselves close now perhaps only contiguous now. In this area wild boar foxes and badgers are at home and on the other hand the birds present include blackbirds and wood pigeons. And what is the relationship between identity and struggle. C shook his head with an incredulous air as the taxi was pulling into the airport. It's not that difficult to understand me. Why are you so bloody difficult. You simply arrive at a point in which everything seems the same but nothing is very important anymore. All around everything was immersed in the silence of dawn. I haven't got any more money. Give me a ring sometime. Have you seen how strange the landscape is. At the entrance on the left there is a rock whose shape reminds you of a dragon's head. Do you see what I want from you. I don't understand anything anymore.

He was a well-built man and had much broader shoulders than men who are five foot nine normally have. Which you could enjoy more fully if you did not spend hours and hours on the phone but got out and looked for more real relationships. I'm not asking you to name names. The fall of that unitary ideological tension. Talking excitedly or angry exclamations. Violence toward inanimate objects. Shattering of so many generous illusions. Unkind sarcastic retorts. Reappearance of traditional weaknesses and old historical legacies under intellectual and moral bodies that had not been capable of fostering a real historical consciousness. Nausea or butterflies in your stomach. Hasty withdrawal from the room. The sky is pale toward the east before the rising of the sun whose rays are refracted in an area of white clouds rising in strata or tufts that increase forming dense dark masses.

Let's try with other pictures. Let me see. I can't see. Something's not right. Don't touch. It has been programmed in such a way that it can never ever deprogramme itself. Now we're starting to see something. Try and understand. The colours start coming out too. They spent the whole afternoon searching for something that had even the slightest resemblance to the description C had given them. The sky was completely blue without a cloud and the sun was starting to blaze. I'm hungry said C is there anything to eat. A meeting that is never consensus and is continuously traversed by the necessity of betrayal. She stretched her legs and glared at him defiantly. I can't remember anything anymore. I'll do my best he answered with mild embarrassment. He had never been in such an uncertain situation. The problem now is what to put to get more light. You can't do any more than that.

Otherwise all that would become impossible. You're seeing other women aren't you she asks and starts slipping her feet into a pair of low-heeled gold sandals. A cat runs from one row of parked cars to the one in which I find myself. The wetlands in the N host a considerable concentration of wild orchids as well as numerous species of migratory birds in the contest of evocative beauty. Trust is for fools. So I jumped into the car closed the door I leant out of the window and burst out laughing. I haven't the foggiest what you're talking about you must be drunk. The sound of his bare feet went off down the corridor. His arms remain still hanging by his sides. We could do with something completely different. It is necessary to see other pictures. A part of the ritual included the etching of figures and writing on the cave wall. My heart is beating fast. He poured himself a drink and headed toward the veranda.

The thing that does not work in this country is the absence of the spirit of revolt. No new ideas coming from the young. They follow in their forefathers' footsteps trying to do better than them. While the thing that counts is always the breaking away never the progress made. He downed his drink and while the waiter was bringing him another he looked at me with anxious eyes as if I were the only friend he had left. The anxiety of an era yet to come that rises to a principle of unconditional liberty to pure energy of dissent. A long silence followed. There was no need to add anything else. In that period C appeared particularly troubled without apparent reason. I decided to drop in to see her without telling her. On arriving at the top of the stairs he stopped to catch his breath. Wherever she looked black clouds heavy with rain filled the sky up to the line of the horizon.

At this point I go back to thinking I have a marina before me as I did earlier instead of a landscape with rather rough water but still the cloudy sky and the sun only shining patchily as it is diffuse light. He walked to the window in his bare feet and pressed his forehead and nose against the tepid glass breathing slowly. As not only is sufficient light desirable but also high sharpness of outline and a certain brightness which are vital for the rendering of the picture. Nevertheless there is no trace of colour. The reason for this should be sought in the water itself because of the dispersion of light in general and the assortment of material in suspension. She sat down again on the bed. In my experience the maximum shooting distance is approximately five metres. He moved downwards his head fell back onto the pillow.

Due to this the shooting distance is considerably shorter than the breadth of view. The path sloped gently down then curved and followed the torrent which was nearly totally hidden from view by the thick broom and hawthorn bushes that grew on its banks. The road rises after a few hundred metres and climbs the hill with frequent bends giving increasingly vaster visions of the lake. With both nostrils closed and focusing on the tip of your nose hold your breath for as long as you can. Outside the window the light was diffuse and soft. He confusedly thought that the blanket had been in the other room since the morning. Relax your arms abruptly. She pulled the sheet up to her chin hung up reached out and caressed his cheek. All interest is accentuated in the harmonious relationship between the curvature of the thighs and that of the abdomen.

Where have you been. She makes it all up. Creeping thyme Thymus serpyllum the horned poppy of the Alps Papaver alpinum var. achantopetala the bitter Nordic buttercup Ranunculus acer borealis there are still a few examples of Thalictrum alpinum the Atragene alpina var. sibirica in the Alps. Until you've had enough. Hereinafter this word was sufficient to produce a contraction of the arteries. Her normally low and husky voice trembled a little. They were advancing with great speed and they soon found themselves within earshot. He started moving faster. We set off an hour later and we got out at the hotel in C. I'll call you if you like. While you are on the telephone you think about how time flies how you have a thousand things to do. It was definitely different at C's. She is lying on the settee with the telephones on the floor constantly moving. She can't come.

Languidly undulating surfaces lack of watercourses the frequent outcrops of rocks that emerge from the fine layer of red earth which nonetheless supports rich crops. The scar on her stomach was visible in the faint dusk light. I'm so happy you came. Let's try another position. Where the rules are not the game. This is how the problem of identity presents itself. He picked up his glass from the floor. A mosquito was buzzing near his ear. It's all like a game. It doesn't feel like time is passing. Don't switch off the light. He closes his eyes then opens them again in order to look in a different direction. Struggle is inherent in identity and without struggle there can be no identity. Inside you can go down into a great cavern in the centre of which there is a rock surmounted by a giant stalagmite. He felt better immediately. What are you doing. Guess what comes next.

While she says this C gets up lifts his arms again still holding his glass in his hand and turns from one side to the other. A fearless man is I think a fool. Cars raced down the main road their tyres screeching. I'm pretty hungry I say. At the end of the built-up area a straight stretch of road starts that runs amongst fields of fruit and vegetables then through the odd olive grove and finally into the reclaimed land. Pulling it toward him in order to continue driving it toward ever-new shores and questions. The clock in the hall strikes 22.30. She has her blonde hair pulled back by a silver clip tanned skin from her life by the seaside luminous teeth. Nothing new under the sun. C had slept nearly the whole journey. Perhaps I should kiss her again. Further off a cargo ship slowly advances northward on the line of the horizon. They had nothing else to say to each other.

Speak up. There are still so many things I would like to know about you. Opening an abyss in human affections is dangerous. I could name names. There was a strange accent in her voice that I had never heard before. She pulled herself away from the window and came toward me smiling. Light was pouring into the room. They were all names I didn't know. The day passed quickly there were still many things to do. C had just fallen asleep when the telephone rang repeatedly. Occasions like this will probably never happen again he thought. You could hear the sound of the sea and the breaking of the waves. Sudden postponements of a meeting that is never agreement but a zigzagging path of convulsive truths. Thanks for calling. Then she said goodbye to me and hung up. I haven't the foggiest idea about what's happening out there. When she had finished reading she tore the letter up and threw it away.

Then she raises the packet a little and offers it to C who shakes his head. That which happens when a woman goes out with a man. What are you thinking about. Fifth symptom the lack of affection so ignore the emotional storms and the upheaval of passion. We have calculated too short an operating period to try to analyse the seasonal changes. Neither the edges of the fields nor C which should appear a little to the left of the centre of the picture are visible while the lighter region toward the right has a surprising aspect. Let me have a look at you. I'm happy you arrived before the others. Despite this restriction the number of details observed was sufficient to draw some conclusions. Since the natural linear characteristics should not appear straight over long distances or bisect each other at least one of the ones that are visible in the photograph must be a road.

The problem of maximal shooting distances must again be remembered. If you can put these four in the same position they were in before. Open your hand. Let's try and leave then. Near the window. These distances are actually present in the Mediterranean Sea. Relax abruptly and rest. After a while she sighed got up and went into the water. She wanted to have a swim but decided it would be better to telephone C straight away. At the time we were only living off the money I was bringing in. The big toe on my right foot hurts and so I try and walk on the outside of my foot. He paid for the taxi took the suitcase up to the room and unpacked the clothes with the typical care and orderliness of a man who is used to living on his own. He looked around. The C airship is missing. Close the window. And you better pull this stuff here out. He closed his eyes so as not to think.

A moment later he heard her moving the coat hangers and closing the creaky door. He was groping his way across the room toward the light switch. C came back after ten minutes and sat down near her. She moved away impatient and sat on the bed her hands on her knees. Again no one spoke for a minute or two. The minutes were ticking away C wondered whether she should leave but she had the feeling that he wanted her company. C switched the light off muttering to himself. A raised open hand as if to stop the person you are addressing. When you moved in with C did he ever talk to you about money. As he walked by the bed he trod on something that was warm squelchy and smooth. Her thighs were two parallel lines which then terminated. The chest is in exactly the same place as it was before. It wasn't there before. Then it started to drip.

So that the same chests that are found below follow its labyrinthine approach to a certain degree. Then you hear a tap at the door. C climbs over her and goes toward the chests. Raise your head shoulders chest and both your legs as high as you can. C calms down temporarily. It concerns three different movements not a single continuous movement. Lying on the ground forehead down legs together hands under his body at shoulder height palms on the floor. They kissed again slowly then he left her. C put her arms around his neck and they kissed passionately. Lying on the ground forehead up knees bent on the floor arms facing slightly out. C stretched out and the sheets suddenly dropped forward. In the end he fell back onto the pillows. Push your torso against the floor tensing your abs and the muscles in your back.

She had vowed to get dressed and do her makeup with special care however probably due to the tiredness of those last two days she had slept all morning. Getting up and putting on her jumper. She carefully hung up her long evening dress again took off her tights her slip opened the window slightly and went to bed. And now we need to start again. From this last series we have chosen the pictures that interested us because they offer a greater probability of discovering signs of life. From that point it extends along the circle of the ramparts and quickly reaches the nearby junctions. Vice versa other light lines intertwine with one another and do not seem to be clearly connected with the system of the currents we have especially focused our attention on these.

You have never written to me said C. She got up opened the door. All of a sudden she went back and sat down in front of the mirror and opened the little bottle. C is living under such mental pressure that he virtually has to speak aloud most of the time. The minutes were ticking away slowly. He walked on the grass between the trees. She was bursting with joie de vivre while she was chatting with the two girls by her side who were laughing at something she had just said. I suddenly felt concerned for C and I breathed a sigh of relief when I saw her again. She came back with a letter that had arrived while we were in C. Well get a move on. In this view I was not able to make out anything more than I had seen in the previous one. Upon reading these various extracts they not only seemed to me irrelevant but I could perceive no mode in which any one of them could be brought to bear upon the matter in hand.

Nevertheless we are almost certainly talking about a natural peninsula. Nevertheless many inorganic substances also display the same type of spectrum and the simple observation of this phenomenon does not appear sufficient to show the existence of vegetation. I'd have got there by now. Body tension. The whole body vibrates the head clearly stands out the arched back extends from its extremity and the tension of the arms drawn diagonally continues from the line of the back. No other sound except that of the water falling on their two entwined bodies. Then you start again. Then silence. She touched his face. He brushes her eyelids with his fingertips. She turned toward him. So what do you want to do he started. It gives me great pleasure. He asked her out he took her to C he had intimate relations with her and he even proposed to her.

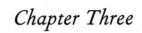

Chapter Three

She saw a thin young man with olive skin wearing a polo neck and a sports jacket and a stocky man with brown hair come out. She heard the car door slam. His slim arms covered in dust from work can be seen under the rolled-up sleeves of his thick blue jumper. The lights were not visible from outside. The view from the top of the hillock of C on the western side of the island dominates the vast expanses of the beautiful countryside that regularly alternates between tilled fields and woods. The easiest indication that we should be able to see for the uncropped terrestrial vegetation should come from the seasonal changes and precisely from the trees of the temperate zone whose leaves change colour and then fall. The lights were on in the rooms on the ground floor. The temperature had dropped noticeably during the night. I came back on the 46. I stopped the car in front of a house and got out.

There the vaults were composed of compact non-porous limestone which was totally covered with tiny lime crystals from the condensation. When I arrived C was already ready and waiting for me. She always said she preferred not to make too many plans. They weren't even the same. And did you have intimate relations with him. No. When did you first meet. He had rolled his sleeves up too and his hands moving back and forth contrasted with her fragile ones. We have especially focused our attention on these. He looked like he was going to sing a song. And then. She accompanied him to the door and said goodbye to him on the doorstep. Big black clouds almost covered the whole of the sky. In the next chapter we shall examine the different types of clouds and their origins. It's all written. Then slowly very slowly the precise meaning of those words started to enter his head.

What are we going to do there. You start from scratch every time. You need to choose. You decide. You just have to decide together. He took another book from the chest opened it randomly and read the first sentence his eyes fell on. Processes change and while old processes and old contradictions disappear new processes and new contradictions emerge and the methods of resolving contradictions differ accordingly. C had had enough of waiting. Why are you so bloody difficult. I know myself well enough. For once I thought I had got it. I think if you're like that you live better you are and you remain more alive. I'm hungry too. She looked at him as if she were seeing him for the first time. He felt a strange emotion wash over him. Airships move very slowly. C was becoming more and more impatient. Let's get a move on now. The same movement is a contradiction.

The test is repeated the following day. Tearful blank bright eyes. Cold hands arid lips. Feeling of warmth. She moved away impatient and sat on the bed her hands on her knees. She lets go of the shutter suddenly went back into the room and lay down on the bed. She sits on the edge of her chair leaning forward. She goes through the wardrobe pushes aside some clothes. He was a well-built man and had much broader shoulders than men who are five foot nine inches tall normally have. It looks like it might be a seaside scene even though the jetty has gone and it gives the impression of a stretch of land emerging out of the water that is rough and reflects a little sunlight and the sunlight filters through the clouds. It is well known that a strong colour contrast compared to the surrounding regions makes the road easy to see even though its width is inferior to the theoretical resolving power.

And though keeping his lively mood his enthusiasm his mobility is imbued with melancholy imagination. Everyone tells me that. And so his compulsive ardour is reined in by anxiety for the future and the spreading of his generosity is limited by a realistic sense of contingency. It is difficult to admit we are not coherent with ourselves in every aspect of our personality. Do you want to know more. I'd like you to be more with it. She stretched her legs and glared at him defiantly. C had told him once that if he went on in this vein he would run the risk of being misunderstood. She carried on undressing not listening to his words. Each on his own. It's obvious that the story couldn't go on like this. Going forward you will realise how accurate his predictions had been. It is strongly advised to read the book right to the end. Going forward it becomes more and more gripping.

A part of the ritual included the etching of figures and writing on the cave wall. Signs that are surprised and cut by the vital system of the current communication. In this sense the various fragments constitute an interior design in which the structure is still that of a door. This fulfils the univocal function of separating or putting in touch. Silence had fallen in the room. You could hear a door slamming in the distance. The scene was completely deserted now. A horizontal association that unleashes fresh vitality that revives the dead. Soon after that C came out of the bathroom covering himself with a yellow towel. I feel more relaxed today it may have been this morning's walk. Would you like a little more tea. If you want to go go. He looked up toward the hill and then down to the dock and the lake. I don't agree that people can't change. Oh shut that door at least.

They contended that a thing can keep on repeating itself as the same kind of thing but not change into anything different. They ascribed the causes of social development to factors external to society, such as geography and climate. Denying that the development of things is determined by their internal contradictions. They had not understood that first and foremost a concrete analysis of the concrete situation is needed to really change things. She took other books from the chests and placed them on the top shelf. Our generation however preferred dealing with practical things. What's there to eat. We could carry on tomorrow said C. By then almost all the chests were empty. While the thing that counts is always the breaking away never the progress made. A book fell on the floor and C did not bend down to pick it up. I'm having trouble following you. He started talking again while C was listening to him carefully.

Dark blue of the panorama. That's right pan out. With the number 6 shoot that mosquito that's there after the long shot. Get the sheet out of the pan shot. Close-up. It's not working. The first are already at their peak in '46. Tell me when. Put a piece of cardboard with a hole in the middle and do it a bit less. Just a little. A little less. Stop. Because it gains transparency. If anything black is easier. The moment the shift occurs the white becomes dominant and the black background and so on for every subsequent change. Continue this check for three minutes. It looks like an X-ray of a fish. It turns into something else here. She raises her head turning her eyes elsewhere. She said there was no more time. It should be number 47 now. The solution is perhaps made easier by the fact that the chest oscillates when you touch it. Nothing. Suddenly a second. Now pull it all off. So why doesn't the eaglet come down.

Let's suppose everything happens just like it does in reality that my body is a system of sense organs in relation with the central organ C. Have you finished the drawing. All the rest has been eliminated. Nevertheless it does not follow a straight course and does not strongly contrast with the surrounding environment. Do you want to show your drawing or not. The third one is not finished. No not in this scene. In this effect they leave together. Written. I think she should go. Let's try and leave then. Now C is all right. If you can put these four in the same position they were in before. And you better pull this stuff here out. So we've done 44 45 this is 46. Then all the rest C something like this. Cut to the chase. Let's continue. Let them write in the meantime. What do those fleeting marks mean. The others are on full blast. They are all on full. You feel as though the part on the left were an X-ray.

We got out at the C hotel and we went up to our room. He went back into the room and closed the door. Then she moistens the brush slightly and dips it into the cosmetic. Let it dry for a few minutes then touch up again with the brush and the cosmetic. She was clutching her hands to her chest careless of her newly-polished nails. Brief pause. His face is very pale he does not seem adequately nourished for such an unspeakable expenditure of energy. He has a considerable ability to attract attention and influence others although they distrust him a little. He stops suddenly at the end of a narrow street. From the window. He had already thought enough about it. Firstly simply relax and note down how many seconds the black part remains dominant and the white part the background. She raised her wrists with her fingers tensed so they would dry. She was lying on the bed leafing through a magazine but could only read a few sentences here and there.

It is possible to reach the bottom bare-footed where there are beautiful deposits. You will find there an ossiferous breccia with bones broken intentionally. I really don't care what they think about me. Her friends had advised her to be more prudent too. A very accurate drawing in its details. It is a mechanism that once started becomes unstoppable so it should be used very prudently. I've never seen anything like it. There 's nothing to laugh about. I had hoped I would make it this time. Anyway said C don't you think that one is master to do what he wants with his own life. She would always repeat the same thing to me. I'm so happy you came. The day passed uneventfully after the trip to the cave and lunch by the seaside. In the internal part of the cave along with an abundance of Pleistocene fauna a human Neanderthaloid tooth was recovered.

The wailing of a foghorn out at sea. C now appeared to be in a very good mood. Dense dark smoke was enveloping everything. Within the walls ruins including a building with a rectangular plan overlooking the port and some rooms carved out of the rock along the S side of the cove. Cars raced down the main road their tyres screeching. They reached the theatre quickly. She had stopped thinking about the problems that were tormenting her. The place where meaning is reduced to surface to signified to appearance and image. There was not the slightest movement in the room. It becomes something magical. C stopped turning to him with a puzzled look on her face. Can you see much he asked. How do you feel now. You can see well from here. Passionate embrace during which they both come forward to the front of the stage. How long until it finishes. Almost there.

The process adopted is that of breaking away and tracing the intensity of daily life. When she had finished reading she tore the letter up and threw it away. He thought that an excessive understanding of the process might be harmful. He was worried not seeing her arrive. They are not suitable things for any old reader. I carried on reading carefully. There is no longer the psychological ego that expresses itself there is no longer the individual that reflects the world through his own single consciousness. He saw her turn the corner walking briskly. A character in which the need to take the initiative and have independence clashes with the desire to retreat within one's own circle of private interests. C got into the car and said let's go I'm in a hurry. She wore an orange dress with a white scarf. They got into the lift without talking. It was an old hotel where they had already stayed on other occasions. Why do you do it.

C was uneasy and it didn't take long for him to guess what had happened a few minutes earlier no more than half an hour earlier. He went on until he could hear the sound of water beneath him. Then he got into his car parked by the kerb a white car. She was exhausted. She thought about C and realised that the difference consisted in a different way of behaving toward things and people. For example C would always say that people couldn't change. Last symptom the characteristic sexual handicaps. C told her they had to come back. All around the landscape was immersed in darkness. Nevertheless many inorganic substances also display the same type of spectrum and the simple observation of this phenomenon does not appear sufficient to show the existence of vegetation. Averting eye contact. He crossed the hall again climbed the stairs and went back into his room.

You should lift it up more open it more with the yellow one. The crudely carved fingers seem to thrust into the abdomen. It's oversimplified. What's wrong you're tense. All right then let's do this. That finished or in the meantime. Then C in the meantime. I had said that we would get those ones there to go down to zero. Now you let them drop and leave them at mid-height. I'm going to carry on. Go on. The C airship is missing. You come down with this thing the mammoth. Why don't you come down. Nobody can help me. Zero blue where 's the mammoth under the skyscrapers. Outside the window the light was diffuse and soft. He went over to the window without speaking. The dark green shutters were half closed to keep the morning sun at bay. He looked around. They were all moving. The matter in hand obliges me to focus mainly on the concluding events.

He was a robust man of average stature from the knitting of the sutures of the cranium and the wear of the teeth we can deduce that he was about twenty-eight to thirty years old. The loads are usually carried by women because it is said that they have stronger heads. Together with his companions using pits he would capture mammoths. His clothes did not survive but the way the numerous mammoth-tusk ornaments are laid out allows us to reconstruct the shape of the waistcoat and trousers. Mammoths and reindeer would wander the cold steppes in the rare conifer woods and with them lived bison wild horses hares arctic foxes. If you are very lucky you might even see a bear but you're more likely to come across a few shy lost hedgehogs. The sun is hidden behind the clouds through which its light filters. The lines reach up as far as the tip of the pole and there they stop abruptly.

It's a landscape with very diffuse sunlight. We are talking about something other than tools made of stone and bone works of art including an ochre-coloured equine figure made from mammoth tusk. The second skeleton was found in an oval-shaped burial place on a layer of coals sprinkled with light red ochre powder. Yet there were brown stains on her t-shirt. C disappears. It is clear that the horizon is completely dark and you can just make it out vaguely. In a great number of cases the solution almost entirely depends on the analysis of the place or position. The landscape as a whole makes me think of two possibilities. There is a mass of light clouds near the centre of the landscape with clouds that slowly become darker as they go toward the horizon. The hippo is out of here. What an effect we 're C. Change scenes the hippo disappears.

However the end has a totally different tone almost an operatic tone. Can I proceed with my project. He told me about it. As is well known this reflex is characterised in newborn babies by a dorsal extension of the big toe while in more mature individuals it is marked by a plantar flexion. This unwanted phenomenon can be contrasted with very shiny paper. Evidently the light I had observed from the bottom and I had first explained as a reflection may be a tree-lined avenue or something like that. I'll show you a detailed plan at the appropriate moment. Follow another silence. Accompanying C to the gate. C pale and thin has entered from the side door strutting like a catwalk model. At six C came down to the bar and ordered vodka with tonic water and a slice of lemon.

All of a sudden she went back and sat down in front of the mirror and opened the little bottle. I set the notepad back down on the very low coffee table in front of the fireplace. She fell back onto the pillow and lay there gazing up at the ceiling. He had a limp in his right foot. It's not cold anymore. At a certain point. They walked together on the pavement where the sun was not shining until the end of the street. She continued but she had to stop again a little bit further ahead at some traffic lights. She walks slowly on the paving streaked by the sun. It wasn't raining. C is living under such mental pressure that he virtually has to speak aloud most of the time. After C had joined her she started getting undressed. C opened the other door to the bathroom softly and entered a room that was exactly the same as hers.

He woke up at about one thirty left his room and most likely lowering himself along the façade reached the balcony on the sixth floor and through the bathroom window entered the house. He got up from the settee and came up to me from behind while I was looking out of the window. She stopped again stubbed out the cigarette she had just lit and you finish the tea that was left in the cup. She was by the fire in front of everyone. A little way off C was looking out of a window. She puts down the cup and lights a cigarette. Instead now she was looking at C who was still talking. He 's standing behind her. No one else gave you any money in that period of time. Both had relations with the two girls. Some weeks passed and they met in C's house again to discuss the new situation that had been created. She suddenly stopped so as not to give away more than she wanted.

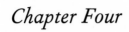

Chapter Four

Definitively disposed of in 1945 by the conservative forces that had already laid a solid base for conserving the old state. Long pause. All my friends have stayed the same they haven't changed a bit but things have changed they have gone in a different direction while we were chatting about all our nice little plans. C shrugs. She gets up wearily. These successes feel they should be due to a society that should have collapsed under their revolutionary impulse and that has instead turned around slowly without them in spite of their opposition on the contrary involving them little by little in a series of ties that did not seem very binding but had quickly become indispensable the new applications the new career prospects the new consumer goods a better standard of living. The telephone rings. Sarcastically. Without that much enthusiasm. She laughs nervously.

Then because of the very nature of things we shall in the end witness a raising of consciousness which moreover is very limited. Evidently the light I had observed from the bottom and I had first explained as a reflection may be a tree-lined avenue or something like that. Did you have intimate relations with him? Yes. She stops talking and dives onto the bed. Have you got anything to say. He looked like he was going to sing a song. He 's always got new things to add. I could not add anything here other than my previous observations. But I realised he was no good for me because I would only really be able to live if I managed to get rid of him. However the end has a totally different tone almost an operatic tone. This implies the movement of the head the torsion of the torso a general contraction and an acceleration of the pulse and respiration.

The phone call the previous night had set the alarm bells ringing. Do you think I want to kill myself. C would always say that there was time to die. He was starting again trying to concentrate better when he heard the by now familiar buzzing and the resonant metallic noise. You need to choose. He was really upset when he found out that C had no intention of coming back. She hangs up before I can even say ciao. He decided to do neither of the two things. She wasn't in the best of moods. He carried on reading lying at the foot of the bed with his head resting on two pillows. At what point do we as individuals prefer to die than to compromise and live. Reading produced a continuous feeling of uneasiness. Each time he gave a different version of the story. A reader is himself a superposition of different states. That very day he went to catch the train to return to town.

She took a sip. The chest is in exactly the same place as it was before. There are more of such chests nearby. They had gone down to the C hotel at about midday they had been on a long walk. From there they had reached C by plane. She goes through the wardrobe pushes aside some clothes. They had booked a room and had left straight away. It didn't taste of anything the glass was warm to the touch as was the liquid that was almost bitter in the mouth. Feeling of warmth. Then it started to drip. The incomprehensibility of action carried out for reasons that no one can comprehend. I haven't been drinking. In your condition. It always happens like that. Nothing ever happens in this town. There 's no more space. Other things are always talked about. Can you see much. You can see. He nervously moved the glass toward the centre of the chest and looked carefully.

He opened another bottle and filled his glass. I'm hungry said C is there anything to eat. He put out his cigarette. Someone like you often thinks that everything might be useless. And though keeping his lively mood his enthusiasm his mobility is imbued with melancholy imagination. She didn't answer his question. It was midday when he got up and started wandering around the house. He opened the drawer and pulled out a pack of photographs. Okay okay I get it. The pictures were in black and white very grainy but quite clear. The wooded point across the bay and further over there the open lake. The building on the riverside. The stonework is made up of small blocks of smooth-faced stone with irregular trapezoidal sections. The interior is decorated with a hook-shaped pattern featuring two colours. And who's this guy on the right with the hat.

Everything changes continuously if we don't notice it is because we have changed too. I don't know what that means. He downed his drink. A vacuum is not a void but rather a teeming mass of these elements that have such a short life. I haven't the foggiest what you're talking about you must be drunk. Honestly I don't want to be one-sided. To be one-sided means not to look at problems allsidedly. At least try and be honest with yourself. I'm being serious and I believe this may be a good starting point. C was trying to talk but couldn't articulate his words. Now beads of sweat form on the back of his neck armpits forehead and cheeks. The end of the cycle. He endeavoured to finish a sentence but his sentences never end. When he left he saw that C was looking down. He remained in that state the whole week.

I saw a flash of hope in his eyes. The anxiety of an era yet to come that rises to a principle of unconditional liberty to pure energy of dissent. Big smiling eyes. He started talking again while C was listening to him carefully. We might be heading toward a catastrophe. She came and sat by him in bed and they both heard the rain hard against the pane of the window. In the veil of shadows he saw the look on her face. He had been waiting for that moment for too long. He carried on talking to hold her attention. Objects in the world are made up of a series of short-lived factors that disappear immediately after their appearance. She sat down on the bed. All things break up into agglomerates of independent and unstable quality and ways of being. Let's hope it stops raining. C changed position on the bed. The red stain on the floor.

Near the window. I feel wonderful tonight. Why not. Nothing. Yes. Oh. What am I going to do with it. Maybe. It doesn't matter. If you want. What do you know about it. It's not easy. I mean it. Do you want me to come. If you've got a mirror I'll show you. With the number 6 shoot that mosquito that's there after the long shot. It looks like an X-ray of a fish. She goes out of the room moving her hips with her head straight she goes toward the exit. C's reflection appears in the mirror. She wrings her hands nervously blinking rapidly. Vague impression of a road and fields with the sunrays diffused through the cloudy sky. She stood still like that waiting for about five minutes perhaps more shivering a little. They meet in a restaurant she smiles at him first. They both had their own flats and sometimes I used to sleep at his and sometimes he slept at mine. I've got some things to pick up.

The road rises after a few hundred metres and climbs the hill with frequent bends giving increasingly vaster visions of the lake. The progression of the sequence is not always the same in terms of time or intensity but it follows a uniform pattern in which approximately three phases of transformation take shape. There is a third type of conflict that occurs when one has set off along a familiar path to pursue a certain end and a new and fascinating opportunity presents itself. It's oversimplified. And then I enjoy it. Have you finished the drawing. Why do you ask. Nothing had changed. The spirit of the Resistance should have become the basis of the Republic but you have failed and are failing in this. He stops to look at him fascinated. It makes me want to laugh.

Then she moistens the brush slightly and dips it into the cosmetic. From that moment the woman's irritability had got worse and had become constant. There is a piece about thirty centimetres wide that sticks out both sides of the screen and has some grey stripes placed vertically all along its length. She pronounced them in her usual subdued and even tone of voice without giving away the slightest emotion. The same thing but more diversified and more scattered. The plants wither as if they were affected by consumption. This view shows a rather weak glimmer of light upward with a strip of dark in the centre and an even weaker and more diffuse light toward the lower part. Forget everything. The water was cold. It comes out at C and continues majestic carved into the plain between lofty wooded terraces feeding numerous irrigation channels at times splitting into many streams.

She was face down and her face was buried in the pillow. Don't move now. C's head moved slightly on the pillow. She pulled the sheet over. He was hugging the pillow. At the restaurant C had managed to make her see that she should not feel tied down because of what had happened. She had ended up believing it. They had slept until midday and had gone to the beach after lunch. It was calm only very little ripples could be made out. It is possible to reach the bottom bare-footed where there are beautiful deposits. A step forward. The cave is divided into two levels one upper and one lower that host a subterranean lake which can be visited by boat. They liked each other but didn't understand each other. He hadn't realised how far you could go. We arrived in C at the dead of night. Guess what comes next. Without going into details. Goodbye C he said but she had already closed the door.

The wailing of a foghorn out at sea. When she woke up she didn't find him by her side. The shells in the drawer had vanished. The new area of changeability is heading to the S giving rise to isolated showers and thunderstorms. I'm pretty hungry I say. Let's go and get something to eat now. They had just finished lunch when the news reached them. The glow of the fires in the darkness of the night and the flashes of the explosions the plumes of smoke. He decided to leave the same day to understand what had happened. He was too shaken by the images he had seen on the screen. The river was flowing calmly clear and fast in the early morning. I accompanied him to the station. All this does not have very much to do with our story but it doesn't matter. We are not obliged to read everything that it is possible to read. A book is endless books and each of them is a slightly different version of you. It's written here.

At the end of the street they could see the white of the house through the trees. His lips were quivering slightly. They went back on the gravel of the path and crossed the threshold. I mustn't act like an idiot again. I don't know why I do it. Why do you do it. To discover a real aspect of reality. She opened the door to the room. She went and sat down in front of the mirror and looked at her profile. There are still so many things I would like to know about you. She turned toward him. It's like we've known each other forever. They had met the previous year at C's house. It had started raining harder. Toward evening the rain seemed to abate. He closed the book and got up from the armchair. It's a book that made me understand the mysteries of life. Do you want to drink something too. I'd like to go back to the city in the next few days. I'm sure my destiny is about to change don't you think so too. Someone knocked on the door.

What wouldn't he have got angry about? If you had relationships with other men. Sticking his hands into his pockets pulling them out straight away one and then the other running his fingers through his hair changing position continuously. He was walking carefully as if the paving hurt his feet. I'd have got there by now. I don't have any more money. C was uneasy and it didn't take long for him to guess what had happened a few minutes earlier no more than half an hour earlier. C had now turned round sweetly so that he was boxed in between her and the rail. And what did he do with your money. If the connexion is to be established it can only be through and by means of a third body. By giving the obstacle different shapes you will in general produce a variation of the possibilities of bypassing and at the same time yes they might be able to grade the difficulty the situation presents.

{45}

We believe we have opened the way not only for the Republican battle but for the total renewal of the Nation's life. The road runs high cutting into the mountain. After having run along the east bank of the lake the road crosses a deep crack at the bottom of which the turbulent waters flow. You feel as though the part on the left were an X-ray. What do those fleeting marks mean. He was still talking when C fell asleep. The right side looks like undeveloped film or a specimen on a slide. The whistle which has the objective of sonorizing the powder works on low-pressure compressed air. What's wrong you're tense. I don't really fancy it that much. Why don't you look at me. Well it looks stupendous. C awoke after an hour and went into the bathroom to get some water. Could you tell me what you are talking about please. Close the window.

The legs are simply formed by straight lines with pointed tips. Of course it could even be a windswept landscape because there are some things that could be trees that have been bent by the wind. The girl drank the whisky says goodnight and leaves. The test is repeated the following day. Today tomorrow or never. Tomorrow is Saturday no tomorrow is Friday. She took a jacket from the wardrobe and put it on. Every now and then you can hear voices coming from the rear of the villa. C came back after about ten minutes and sat down near her. He squinted slightly. A moment later he heard her moving the coat hangers and closing the creaky door. They had left their room toward evening and had departed again by train for C. I told him I really couldn't believe it. How did you get this scar I asked. He took her face in his hands and kissed her.

She washed her hands took off her shoes and went back to gazing out of the window. Equal and symmetrically opposite hands. Sure enough he ran his fingers through his hair to smooth it down a little. All he does is shake his head out of pity but without speaking. C is wearing a tweed jacket with leather elbow patches a light jumper and grey trousers. They heard him lift the telephone receiver and dial a number. The girl's slender body trembled convulsively. The door slams hard behind him. She was rather tidy and seemed much younger than she actually was until you look at her white face with her wan lips and without lipstick impassive and smooth a curiously cold and rigid smoothness. C moves toward the door but once there he halts and stands stock-still for a moment. The telephone rings in the hall. Noise of a train. She sits. Brief pause.

Neither supporting in his internal struggle and when he had reached the peak of his career it was inevitable that he would feel more and more dispossessed and excluded. And when he arrived she had not finished getting dressed yet. She was awoken by a sound of voices by the noise of people walking around the house. She goes into the bathroom finding a warmer environment there and lets the boiling water run into the bath. She carefully hung up her long evening dress again took off her tights her slip opened the window slightly and went to bed. He stopped telephoning and for all the rest of the evening he subjected me to an absurd interrogation. C sat on the edge of the bed switches on the lamp. I was at C's I slept with him. Still leaning on the table as if he were sleeping. Standing struggling to keep his balance he laughs. Pulling himself up just as he is about to fall off the chair. Looking out of the window.

Clear proof that the forest has retreated further south. He said it didn't matter. He had already thought enough about it. Why should I hate. It was definitely different at C's. Later he was putting his hands in freezing cold water after having whispered a word. The same impression as before with the brighter light from above and the area of light in the background that extends toward the edge becoming almost a strip of light along the lower side. It doesn't matter. Please note the absence of conifers. We got out at the C hotel and we went up to our room. She was lying on the bed leafing through a magazine but could only read a few sentences here and there. It is as if it were the photograph of a horizontal tree. In this view I was not able to make out anything more than I had seen in the previous one. Atrocious terrible solitude.

She lets herself fall back toward him. He's standing behind her. Turning round and looking at him in the face. Raising her hands and moving away from him. All I remember is having been scared one day when I met him on the stairs. All imaginable pathways of the line that represents a direct connexion to the objective are equally impracticable and no adjustment of the shape of the body to the spatial forms of the surrounding objects can allow them to reach the objective. Opening his arms. She spins round in a fit of rage. He moves in order to look at her face. He looks around. Moving closer to her. Averting eye contact. One of the first sentences that came to his mind. They suddenly look each other in the eyes. Taking one of her arms. Tremors perspiration weight loss and exophthalmia soon followed.

Chapter Five

The duration of its light is about 1/100 of a second. The determination of the heat liberated coincided by approximately less than 1 per cent with the values that he had calculated in advance based on the oxygen and carbon dioxide measurements. One attacks the psychic function from above the other from below and the analysis of these two ways of dissolution shows us its integration. We have to do specific practical things now stop wasting our time with your utopian dreams. They said nothing else to each other. Who knows what they were talking about there. And then where did they go. He was walking slowly down the street. When they arrive at the airport it is a few minutes to midnight. She opened the door and goes slowly up the entrance steps. She parked the car and flung open the door.

The same subjects in a state of wakefulness constantly responded with a normal inflection. When she woke up she just had enough time to take a shower and drink a coffee not even the time to telephone C. She was awoken by a sound of voices by the noise of people walking around the house. She listened to what he was saying as she was going in and out of the bathroom. Then slowly very slowly the precise meaning of those words started to enter his head. Have you got anything to say. And he said when you would leave. Did you have intimate relations with him? Yes. Every phrase was repeated twice at a distance of time. If you don't mind the question. C carries on answering in a subdued tone. I closed her fist in my hand. Ask me something else if you want. I could only do what he told me. She came and lay down next to me on the settee. In the end he realised it was unbearable.

They had come across very few other cars along the road. A strong wind was blowing. C shook his head with an incredulous air as the taxi was pulling into the airport. He felt much better he had wound down the window and fresh air was coming in. What are we going to do there. C was behaving as if nothing had happened. This contradiction exists in the process of development of all things. I don't really know where this is going. I don't understand what you mean. We decided to face the issue only after our arrival. C hated the reading of novels. He had only brought a few books with him because he hadn't intended to stay long at C. The phone call the previous night had set the alarm bells ringing. He didn't have a clear idea of the next moves to make. Before landing he suggested she stayed calm. I started laughing while I was talking and it worked.

The girl drank the whisky says goodnight and leaves. The fear that I too would judge her without indulgence fuelled that nervousness that immediately exploded in the confession that follows. I told him I really couldn't believe it. It didn't taste of anything the glass was warm to the touch as was the liquid that was almost bitter in the mouth. Moving his hand slowly. The open hand as if to stop the person you want to call. She took a sip. He had read a lot of books on the subject since he had become aware of C's failure but this was the only thing that had provided him with an explanation. Hasty withdrawal from the room. The minutes were ticking away C wondered whether she should leave but she had the feeling that he wanted her company. She took a jacket out of the wardrobe and put it on. She looked out of the window bending forward and stayed in that position for a few minutes.

Her head falls back onto the pillow. Variable cloudiness with scattered thunderstorms. Going forward you will realise how accurate his predictions had been. Things that oppose each other also complement each other. Everyone knew about their story by now. It was midday when he got up and started wandering around the house. He opened the drawer and pulled out a pack of photographs. They spent the whole afternoon searching for something that had even the slightest resemblance to the description C had given them. A white house on a cliff at the bottom of which the waves break. The coast hides numerous creeks and ravines many of which can only be reached by boat. Few trees in the background. The rain showed no sign of abating. He had given up smoking. He had cancelled the reality but he had to invent another. He no longer had any desire to see anyone. He left closing the door behind him.

And that's how this story ends. His arms remain still hanging by his sides. A person who is scared above all of herself. There was a brief silence during which I noticed a series of different expressions flash across C's face one after the other. You could hear a door slamming in the distance. Now C was trying to talk but couldn't articulate his words. He wasn't afraid of what the consequences of his action would be but feared that once they had got to the bottom of it things would change unpredictably. One thing transforms into another by means of a leap. It had taken him quite a long time to understand. He had red eyes and a pale face. Her blue blouse was all creased. I can't go on like this. I tried to get her to understand that she really had to change her life. The metal cable was drawn taut and then a crash was heard. A noise of footsteps that went off into the night.

The aeroplane coming in to land. The earth appeared to be furrowed by deep gullies. The passengers rushed toward the exit. Crossing the old town he remembered the night at the theatre. Dead boring. The memories of the past brought to light by the archaeological digs by the majestic medieval monuments are numerous. Everyone needs their past he thought. On arriving at the top of the stairs he stopped to catch his breath. He had hung all his hopes on that meeting. He wondered whether C really missed him and had a moment of angst. All I want is you I whispered to her. In the veil of shadows he saw the look on her face. I know he replied to me quietly. His head falls back onto the pillow panting. They had not understood that first and foremost a concrete analysis of the concrete situation is needed to really change things. They lay in each other's arms for a long time without talking. It was raining outside.

It doesn't matter. The sun high on the horizon and entirely or partially hidden by the clouds through which the rays filter in a characteristic way. There is now a rather brief allusion to two secondary characters in the affair. Her face shows great pain. One last detail should remain unsaid. Her contorted body lay on the sofa in front of the fireplace. The sun filtering through the shutters streaked her hair and tanned arms changing the colours of her dress. C pushed back a tuft of hair that was falling in his eyes and continued. She has snow-white skin and straight hair falling to her shoulders. He holds her tight by the waist and shoulder stroking her long red hair then went back and sat down on the edge of the bed. I was so happy. She slowly crossed the room in C's direction. Her face was flushed almost triumphant. Biting her lower lip. Thinking about the scene that has just taken place.

The path sloped gently down then curved and followed the torrent which was nearly totally hidden from view by the thick broom and hawthorn bushes that grew on its banks. The wind has entirely ceased but it is evident that we are still hurrying on to the south under the influence of a powerful current. She chose a patch of shade under the branches of the tree next to C and stretched out calmly on the dry grass that pricked her skin through her light dress. So we've done 44 45 this is 46. I'll have to proceed only with references and reminders that knowing the texts can be integrated. The progression of the sequence is not always the same in terms of time or intensity but it follows a uniform pattern in which approximately three phases of transformation take shape. Do you want to see the drawing or not. Everything has been thoroughly studied and all obstacles foreseen.

She makes it all up. He said it didn't matter. Round the corner the sun shone in your eyes and the air was warmer. He had a limp in his right foot. The hand loosens its grip. All the chests are empty. Brief pause. The water was cold. I went back up on the bridge being careful not to slip on the oily iron ladder. We still held on to the southward without any very great impediments. In latitude 82°20'N longitude 43°5'W the sea being of an extraordinary dark colour we again saw land and upon closer scrutiny found it to be one of a group of very large islands. They were advancing with great speed and they soon found themselves within earshot. In the four canoes which might have been fifty feet long and five broad there were 110 savages in all.

The perpetual mobility of a desire of a dream without time or space. It doesn't feel like time is passing. I really don't care what they think about me. In the film after all the story of the title is almost secondary and the leading actors lack charm nobility sensuality. It might even be another story. Another drink. C asked me to stay that night too. He switched off the light and went to the window and looked outside. C tenderly shushed him then she started to sing. Her arms were soft and lithe. It was a song I knew and she sang it well. The lower half of her body was illuminated by the yellow moonlight. Move over a bit. That's better. Bit more. That's enough now. She pulled the sheets over. At this point she told him everything. She had never spoken about it with anyone. I spent all night trying to remember her every word.

They let the telephone ring and ring without answering it. Where should you start. While she says this C gets up lifts his arms again still holding his glass in his hand and turns from one side to the other. She couldn't finish the sentence. Her story weaves and unweaves like the tapestry she was working on. The frame is well proportioned and costs in a range between genuine borders. The only thing I need is something I can really believe in. The central strip has a pattern of beautiful flowers embellished with leafy stems and small buds. How do you feel now. The new area of changeability is heading to the S giving rise to isolated showers and thunderstorms. I wanted us to have a few days and nights to be together on our own. The borders bear a continuous pattern of plant shoots with small flowers and an abundance of blooms interchanging their direction. The flight was going to depart in less than an hour.

C raced in waving his arms and shouting something that she did not catch. He closed the book and got up from the armchair. What you read might seem quite random. There was a strange accent in her voice that I had never heard before. She wore an orange dress with a white scarf. She had not expected him to come back so quickly. He had not had the time to understand what was happening. The other possible interpretations are endless but at the moment this is the only reality that belongs to us. He carried on complaining we never do anything together I don't know a walk. He lit another cigarette. I haven't come back to hear the same old stories he said peevishly. Now leave me alone. I have to go said C it's going to be a tough day tomorrow. This little episode was then forgotten without any problems.

One day they went to C together and when the other guests left C told her that she would have to stay with him. He got up from the settee and came up to me from behind while I was looking out of the window. Her straight red hair came to her shoulders. The dominant colours of the old town of C are the bright red of the bricks and the pale green of the copper covering the roofs and the domes of the bell towers. Neither the edges of the fields nor C which should appear a little to the left of the centre of the picture are visible while the lighter region toward the right has a surprising aspect. She waits still like that for about three minutes shivering a little. My husband came toward me I was scared he was going to beat me I covered my face with my hands. He moves in order to look at her face. Tremor sense of weakness. Moving closer to her. She was furious and a wave of rage rose from her neck to her ears.

And as we are ten years younger and haven't had to live through the tough war years we can't accept these cop-outs. A strange sense of solitude and aloofness from the whole world took hold of C. Relax your arms abruptly. The arms increase the length of the body and the hands appear to be under the lower limbs. The girl turned and C was able to contemplate her slender figure amidst that sea of flowers. Going to the left without getting close to the row of poles is dangerous. I had said that we would get those ones there to go down to zero. Yeah but I don't know how they do it. The outline of the beams looked silvery under the large blue lamps. When they had arrived at the peak C suddenly stopped. C was walking by her side in silence. Could you tell me what you are talking about please. And you were talking about money. We did.

I'm willing to do anything to help him. From the open door I saw the meadow that slowly turns light blue and then silvery. The sun is hidden behind the clouds through which its light filters. He starts talking to her gently. Together with his companions using pits he would capture mammoths. He had walked for hours and hours before reaching the river. From here the narration proceeds more quickly and confidently. One day he saw a boat pass with quite a few men on board which however vanishes out of his sight before he can make himself seen. C turned her head in the direction of the voice. Talking excitedly or angry exclamations. Tearful blank bright eyes. The women's hands like those of the men lie still after the long daily climbs. I've skipped a passage. A few seconds later we were on the beach.

The following morning they met at C. What was in those drawers. C casually asked her where she had put the shells he had seen the year before in her house. C laughs provoking him and runs away. C put her arms around his neck and they kissed again for a long time passionately. C remained still without answering. Out of the blue a few days later they decide to go back to town. A few weeks later she realised she was pregnant. Just as long as they don't ask you where you've been. It's easy to miss it so you should keep your eye on the right-hand side of the road. When the taxi arrived we left for the station and we took the train to C. He drove very prudently. They kissed again slowly then he left her. Noise of a train. It's a landscape with very diffuse sunlight. What an effect we're C. Not so fast.

Looking out of the window. I saw C race past in a taxi. Three streets all of which are lined by trees can be seen. Big black clouds almost covered the whole of the sky. Vice versa other light lines intertwine with one another and do not seem to be clearly connected with the system of the currents. He lit a cigarette. A strong smell of smoke hung in the room. Not far from C's great hall with its central pillar of rock there is a shallow chamber where stands a large stone wall that is more than twenty metres wide. One of the wardrobe doors was open and C noticed that there were fewer women's clothes hanging there than the other time. The blouse had wide sleeves long and gathered in at the wrists. Quickly opening and closing all the wardrobe doors. In the next chapter we shall examine the different types of clouds and their origins.

Upon reading these various extracts they not only seemed to me irrelevant but I could perceive no mode in which any one of them could be brought to bear upon the matter in hand. I feel so unhappy and I really want to die. I set the notepad back down on the very low coffee table in front of the fireplace. From that moment the woman's irritability had got worse and had become constant. As a result of the abundant wealth of phyto and zooplankton also aided by the slimy riverbed there live numerous species of fish some of which are native others have been introduced to the waters including the lake whitefish the char the pike the shad the carp the tench the bleak the European chub the eel and the trout which are extremely sought after for their excellent meat and may reach a considerable size. A thought suddenly strikes me. It was no longer a simple hand rail but a metal cable charged with electricity that arrived as far as the platform. The lake and the road could be seen from there.

Raising her hands and moving away from him. She looked into my eyes. She glared at him as if it were of little importance. So what do you want to do he started. How he had changed. She thought about C and realised that the difference consisted in a different way of behaving toward things and people for example C would always say that people couldn't change. She had believed once. Instead now she was looking at C who was still talking. They went on like this for a good half an hour. Then that story of their unambiguous simple straightforward relationship. It's no good for defending yourself or fighting against anything. He couldn't see anything else because a veil of cloud had covered the whole landscape. To have fun. One sentence after another. She knew she would finally leave him for C sooner or later and this was the whole story.

Chapter Six

She kept on thinking about him while C walked up and down the room. She has a confident air about her as she deals with the books she takes them from the chests reads the titles and quickly places them on the bookshelves. Hence we can acknowledge that a perfect similarity of colour with a certain background does not on its own constitute camouflage at all. One month later C telephoned in the dead of night. She was the only person who would comfort me showing me love consideration affection. They crossed the wide pavement and reached the car. We have to do specific practical things now. He set off slowly along the gravel path. And him what did he say. He laughed and got into the car while he was saying. All my friends have stayed the same they haven't changed a bit. He arrived at the big white house with high windows and a steep roof.

We reached the hotel by taxi at about eleven o'clock. He came down into the lobby using the stairs. He had been silent the whole journey. Three streets all of which are lined by trees can be seen. I saw the leaves move slowly. C looks at him through the windowpane. Realising what C said. Getting up and putting on her jumper. Pointing to a guy who was sitting wrapped up in an overcoat. Accompanying C to the gate. Jesting. Racing down the steps of a metro station. The sea was calm and flat and the sun was rising. I continued to walk always treading on the outside part of my foot. I closed her fist in my hand. The blouse had wide sleeves long and gathered in at the wrists. At the end of the street the lights were going on and off. He looked like he was going to sing a song. There was nothing else.

And what am I going to do now. Tears were rolling down his face. I don't think I can start again like I did before. C walks up and down nervously. You start from scratch every time. I don't understand what you mean. C went into the bathroom to look at herself in the mirror. She wasn't in the best of moods. The door opened wide. It's not that difficult to understand me. We can understand each other she said knowingly. He shoved his hands into his trouser pockets. I can't remember the first time we met very well. You could see rain falling in the triangle of light. We used to see each other almost every day. The continuous perpetual stalemate so there are neither winners nor losers. The time before I told her not to come back without the letter. We left the city behind us and we headed toward the coast that was a few kilometres away. I would have liked to have spent more time in her company but I had to get back to town quickly.

He came into the room and headed toward the window. One day he sees a boat pass with quite a few men on board which however vanishes out of his sight before he can make himself seen. You can see a lot. You can see. I had already noticed it but it appeared more evident on her tanned skin. Shattering of so many generous illusions. She mulled over it for a while then she decided to resume the conversation. I had never told her that during our last meeting C had repeatedly claimed he still loved her. She took a sip. They spent most of their time shut up in the room sleeping reading or talking. C could never manage to get up at a decent hour in the morning and didn't have the slightest idea of the value of money. I told him I'd think about it. Nothing ever happens in this town. He reached into the darkness for the bottle.

One must be open to the thing that is being born that is shapeless magmatic it seems like it resembles life. Now we're starting to see something. I don't want to talk about it. Going forward it becomes more and more gripping. They didn't say another word to each other all day. He had cancelled the reality but he had to invent another. The pictures were in black and white very grainy but quite clear. It was often difficult for her to understand if they were moving normally. He watched her head toward the bathroom naked picking up her handbag from the bedside table. The next day I couldn't remember anything about what had happened. The sun was hot the skylarks were singing at a great height. On my way back home the sun was beating down on my face and the people I met turned to look at me. Other pictures flashed on the screen so fast that he could not identify most of them.

When he left he saw that C was looking down. C had stopped telephoning and wandered around the room looking bored. Then she had raced off to lock herself in the bathroom. C had wandered off evidently bored by the turn of events. The sound of his bare feet went off down the corridor. The scene was completely deserted now. He cut himself without realising. She went into the bathroom to look at herself in the mirror. He pulled out a t-shirt from one of the chests stacked up in the bedroom to staunch the blood that was pouring from his face. He thought he heard a sound from the other side of the door but was distracted by his own image reflected in the mirror. I'm not C. A noise of footsteps that went off into the night. She had stopped bleeding. You could see rain falling in the triangle of light. He walked from the door and crossed the street merging into the darkness.

C gazed at the wall but didn't see her. The sudden roar of a plane in the clear sky made him look up. In that period C appeared particularly troubled without any apparent reason. She took other books from the chests and placed them on the top shelf. The silhouette of the body can be clearly seen through the reflection of the lamp in the mirror. She came and sat by him in bed and they both heard the rain hard against the pane of the window. Pulling her gently to himself. C in her pistachio-coloured dress. C put his arms round her waist and pulled her close. All I want is you I whispered to her. The rocks sprayed by the waves. When we remember we are still producing pictures even if the result is set far in the future. C was unable to accompany her on those trips of the imagination. She shook her long shiny black hair behind her back and smiled at me. She had forgotten everything.

She was at the water's edge in a strangely passive position bowed as though she were waiting for something a call or something that might emerge from the water. Our canoes were beached about twenty yards away. Let's go back where we came from. From there or from another place it made no difference. C swimming off describes an arc then he turned coming back in a straight line toward me and got out of the water. It was about ten to twelve. At six o'clock in the evening we had regained the beach our canoe was moored to the usual place and the C rocked in the water two miles from the shore. In my experience the maximum shooting distance is approximately five metres. The sixth time the situation became brighter. Now I feel as fresh as a daisy. A telephone rang twice somewhere and then stoppped. I wake up suddenly in the armchair because the telephone rings.

That flows like fresh water leaving the unsolved problems that are absolutely refractory to the impellent necessities of breaking the mould shown by a society and a culture suffering from traditionalism. It marked the first setback in the momentum that the anti-Fascist struggle the Resistance the Liberation had given the Italian people. When they arrived at the peak C stopped suddenly. Now C is all right. Never losing sight of the matter in hand. Every now and then she opened her mouth wide and I could see her tongue that was moving slightly. The dark green shutters were half closed to keep the morning sun at bay. The outline of the beams looks silvery under the large blue lamps. His head was heavy and he could feel that his lips nostrils and eyelids were puffy. Then all the rest C something like this. The right side looks like undeveloped film or a specimen on a slide.

She came back with a letter that had arrived while we were in C. Finally satisfied with the changes made to the scene he returned to the armchair he had chosen and made himself comfortable with his right foot dangling over the armrest. The events of the last twenty-four hours had been a true test of his intellectual ability and now while it was as if he were paralysed in the moonlight his face reflected a greenish pallor that was not only due to the rays of the moon. In latitude 82°20'N longitude 43°5'W the sea being of an extraordinary dark colour we again saw land and upon closer scrutiny found it to be one of a group of very large islands. Below us there was a plateau of snow stretching out above us a pale sky empty of snow.

She flicked her hand as if she were trying to shoo something away. Surpassing your limits is in reality an unattainable goal. A mosquito was buzzing near his ear. All right all right but now that's enough of this story. C moved her arm in his direction. She was face down and her face was buried in the pillow. Her arms were soft and lithe. He gave her a long kiss on the lips. He didn't have dark eyes as she had thought at first. You could even start from another episode and obtain a slightly different story. For example. He got up and slowly moved toward the door. C raised both his hands his palms open as if he wanted to ask a question. He bowed his head two or three centimetres. The fable of the tortoise and the hare comes to mind. I had a long conversation with C she announced casual as ever. Yet something was telling him that his life was going to get more complicated.

There are vistas of olive groves vineyards lush valleys and mountain peaks at every turn. I didn't want to let him think there would be another occasion. You can spot the mountains and the blue sky from between the trees. Pulling it toward him in order to continue driving it toward ever-new shores and questions. The only thing I need is something I can really believe in. I didn't know how to answer. It's obvious we 're dealing with a different situation here. It becomes something magical. The side of the mountain was covered with bushes and fruit trees covered by pink blossom. There is no meaning but something like a dream of meaning. When she woke up she didn't find him by her side. He glanced at the piles of clothes on the floor and pushed them to one side. His eyes had got used to the darkness of the flat. He decided that he would never undergo such an ordeal in the future.

He lit a cigarette and threw the match out of the car window. The street that led out of town went toward the sea. It was an old hotel where they had already stayed on other occasions. It was a long story that she didn't feel like telling. The day passed quickly there were still many things to do. Toward evening the rain seemed to abate. She reached the balcony and gazed at the blue of the ocean. If only I could understand who I really am. So where the hell are you. C felt herself being overcome by a wave of anger and waited for it to pass before talking. Stick a cork in it. I want to tell you something. She went up to C peeking round the door that was ajar. I'm talking to you. I haven't come back to hear the same old stories he said peevishly. Up there the breeze was cold and invigorating. After all that's happened. In the room the telephone started ringing again and C headed quickly toward the door.

Stamp your feet. Body tension. Clench your teeth and fists. Tremor sense of weakness. Then she lifts her feet and lets herself sink. When she heard the lock of the door connecting the two rooms click she reopened her eyes. There is a dark line in the water that could be a dock or a breakwater or something like that. He woke up at about one thirty left his room and most likely lowering himself along the façade reached the balcony on the sixth floor and through the bathroom window entered the house. At the end of the narrow street the traffic lights are stuck on red. The dominant colours of the old town of C are the bright red of the bricks and the pale green of the copper covering the roofs and the domes of the bell towers. If you continue to drive very fast you can even complete the trip in two and a half days but it is more sensible to give yourself three.

In the darkness the screen emitted a pale light you could hear the soft swishing of the sea in the distance. I looked over toward the bed. What's wrong you're tense. It's oversimplified. Nevertheless it follows a straight course and does not strongly contrast with the surrounding environment. These distances are actually present in the Mediterranean Sea. That finished or in the meantime. Then C in the meantime. And then I enjoy it. Why are you pulling my hair. She was the only person who comforted me showing me love consideration affection. C had stopped he looked about holding his breath. He paid for the taxi took the suitcase up to the room and unpacked the clothes with the typical care and orderliness of a man who is used to living on his own. He looked around. She looked up and looked fixedly at him. The girl turned and C was able to contemplate her slender figure amidst that sea of flowers.

The fall of that unitary ideological tension. This term fills me with horror. Violence toward inanimate objects. There are many examples of such chests in the vicinity. We start looking everywhere in vain until C had the idea of leaving. They'd booked a room and had left straight away. They didn't get in touch with anyone for several weeks. Before leaving her red hair moves briskly and the girl glances over at C who with his big tortoiseshell glasses takes or pretends to take notes in his notepad. He was a robust man of average stature from the knitting of the sutures of the cranium and the wear of the teeth we can deduce that he was about twenty-eight to thirty years old. We can go out now if you want. You need to go back to C and proceed down the 46 for a couple of kilometres until you come to an abandoned sawmill.

The second skeleton was found in an oval-shaped burial place on a layer of cardboard sprinkled with red ochre powder. She was wearing a beige linen dress with a red scarf. From the position of her intertwined fingers we can understand what the people in the place we are talking about were like in that moment. A shape can be transferred to another place acquiring new meaning or maintaining its primary one at the same time. Is that why you're sad. Maybe. Everything goes so many things go you can't even imagine how many now. And they precipitate along with the water onto the walls of the cylinder and then pass into the drain that leads into a collection well for the material. I'm really drunk. He remembered that once many years before they had met C had predicted that one day she would not be able to help leaving her husband.

He had rolled his sleeves up too and his arms moving to and fro contrasted with her fragile ones. And when he arrived she had not finished getting dressed yet. She turns other pages still yawning. When she woke up she just had enough time to take a shower and drink a coffee not even the time to telephone C. He telephoned over and over again and invited her. C sat on the edge of the bed switches on the lamp. The cold water that was touching his body and ruffling his hair made him shiver. She stops talking and dives onto the bed. Then he said that that evening he had returned home late had drunk a lot and had gone to sleep. She had vowed to get dressed and do her makeup with special care however probably due to the tiredness of those last two days she had slept all morning. She told me that we would have to get married sooner or later.

Numerous valleys merge into this including Piumogna Valley that belongs to the Campo Tencia group which is important alpinistically and the Val Bedretto that running along the west coast of the St Gotthard penetrates as far as under the high mounts that surround the head of the Val Formazza and ends at the Nufenen Pass. We reached the peak after two hours. The same thing but more diversified and more scattered. First I filled the glasses then I slowly crossed the meadow up to the pink oleanders that were growing on the riverbank. It comes out at C and continues majestic carved into the plain between lofty wooded terraces feeding numerous irrigation channels at times and splitting into many streams. At first the subject put his hands in freezing cold water and the arteries contracted. A long thin rivulet of water slowly advances on the asphalt. She moves slowly under his body. The woman answered no certainly not. He has never written to me said C.

The buildings that surround the municipal piazza are the very centre of the town where the traffic is heavy at every hour of the day and night. In her bright blue eyes. He would arrive before nightfall without any problem even though the light was already fading. Sticking his hands into his pockets pulling one out straight away and then the other running his fingers through his hair changing position continuously. Stroke my hair. You've been crying. Biting her nails and lips. She looked into my eyes. Let me have a look at you. She looks around. What have you done. Then silence. One sentence after another. All she had to say. I think that's enough. It gives me great pleasure. From start to finish. He brushes her eyelids with his fingertips. He told her that they would go away soon and they would never leave each other again. He smiled weakly. What are you thinking about.

Chapter Seven

She looked up and saw him coming toward the car. There were some flowers in a vase and a long sofa in front of the fireplace. He headed off slowly along the gravel-covered path. He dropped his coat on the chair. The lights were on in the rooms on the ground floor. C turns. He took the street lined by trees. He brushed her cheek with his lips then he kissed her mouth. They crossed the wide pavement and reached the car. Behind him C remained impassive her cheeks a little flushed from tiredness her hands leaning on her knees her head bowed slightly eyes lowered. I've never seen anyone recover so quickly. I haven't been drinking. I'm not sad. I am not that bothered besides it had all been expected anyway. He set their two glasses down on the table and took her hands in his and got her to stand up.

A debate about whether C's identity should be revealed follows. One may even come to the conclusion that she must have died in the autumn. Did you have intimate relations with him. Yes. Realising what C said. Quickly opening and closing all the wardrobe doors. Running up and down all over the room until his strength failed him. She looked in his eyes while she was thinking she would never manage to tell him the truth. She came and lay down next to me on the settee. Because he had total control over my life. I could only do what he told me. She was like that because I was afraid of him. But I realised he was no good for me because I would only really be able to live if I managed to get rid of him. So I left. C pale and thin has entered from the side door strutting like a catwalk model. A small cape of the same colour fell over her shoulders.

He was in no rush to come to the end. An enormous amount of useless words. You simply arrive at a point in which everything seems the same but nothing is very important anymore. The same movement is a contradiction. Nothing ever happens anyway. A sort of nihilism for which he felt a profound fondness. Be careful not to hurt yourself. The only thing to do. At what point do we as individuals prefer to die than to compromise and live. C walks up and down nervously. This contradiction exists in the process of development of all things. I searched everywhere. It rejects the system that is organised by a completed thought and it guarantees the imperfect space of the fragment. I can't find my keys. A fragment anticipates the comfort of a blank and an interruption an illumination and a pause. I don't feel like listening to you anymore. I want to get out of here finally.

Before leaving her red hair moves briskly and the girl glances over at C who with his big tortoiseshell glasses takes or pretends to take notes in his notepad. The lack of affection. The incomprehensibility of action carried out for reasons that no one can comprehend. I told them I would think about it. Without holding out your hand to him she said smiling. I'm afraid it's a bit like this for everyone. C turned her head in the direction of the voice. She smiled at him knowingly then picked up the receiver and dialled a number. And you used to go to bed with other men while you were living with him. Yes with C. I'm not asking you to name names. He asked me to get someone to lend me some money. When you moved in with C did he ever talk to you about money. She sits leaning forward on the edge of the chair. He nervously moved the glass toward the centre of the chest and looked carefully.

She carried on undressing not listening to his words. The last time they had met had been one week earlier on the beach. She didn't answer his question. C looked at himself in the mirror trying to remember what his appearance was like the first time they had met. The first sentence he had said to her. A meeting that is never consensus and remains continuously a path from the necessity of betrayal. They didn't say another word to each other all day. Because this sentence by C had a role in the destiny of his life. Because this shows as if it were on a pedestal the very contradiction of every language. It is a unit of life and her life can be summed up in a few phrases. C was wearing a light dress that came just above the knee. You could play with the ambiguity of the expression and claim that C has spent all his life making sentences. Her head falls back onto the pillow.

To be one-sided means not to look at problems all-sidedly. C had stopped telephoning and wandered around the room looking bored. For example only the favourable conditions but not the difficult ones. The past and not the future. Only individual parts but not the whole. Only the defects but not the achievements. Snow had started falling again more heavily. It means not to understand the characteristics of both aspects of a contradiction. He stopped taking notes and concentrated on what he would have to do in the next few hours. He poured himself a drink and headed toward the veranda. C asked him if he really felt up to going. She was not listening to him anymore. Treat life as if it were a game. He wasn't afraid of what the consequences of his action would be but feared that once they had got to the bottom of it things would change unpredictably. Her body tightens. Oh shut that door at least.

The silhouette of the body can be clearly seen through the reflection of the lamp in the mirror. C's profile in the mirror as she combs her hair. A static composition of static indications of the various positions taken by a shape in movement. A shape that passes through the space through the line. He ardently wanted to kiss her. We have to talk about another practical aspect. That is that the sentence can be structured and so it poses a problem of value. His head falls back onto the pillow panting. They hug it's not a very comfortable position but they stay together and he strokes her hair. We could carry on tomorrow said C. A long silence followed. He could not find another solution. There must be a mistake somewhere. The snowflakes fall slow and wet against the narrow window. We might be heading toward a catastrophe.

As soon as he opened his eyes he saw C. Snuggled up in an armchair. At the foot of the bed he waited motionless for C to awaken. She raises her head turning her eyes elsewhere. She told me that we would have to get married sooner or later. And he said how you would live. She would always say that she didn't have any money but loads of friends. He phoned her again many times and invited her. Ambivalence that is the possibility of feeling hate and love for the same person at the same time. Then with her long tapering fingers she tidies her red hair. She uncrosses her legs that she has kept one on top of the other all along almost tightly clung to by her pistachio-coloured dress. Then they say the two were seeing each other. She goes out of the room moving her hips with her head straight she goes toward the exit. Suddenly C appears in the doorway with a long beard and in his shirt sleeves. Autism that is the conviction of being a superman who is not subject to the laws of society.

The third one is not finished. I think she should go. Only a certain Mr C was talked about but everyone should acknowledge he is one of the main protagonists. At the time we were only living off the money I was bringing in. From the study of the seeds found we can also conclude that it must have died in the autumn. From that moment the political reaction started that should have brought into question the institutional battle itself. It marked the first setback in the momentum that the anti-Fascist struggle the Resistance the Liberation had given the Italian people. And you were talking about money. We did. Never losing sight of the matter in hand. Not in this scene. We believed we opened the way not only for the Republican battle but for the total renewal of the Nation's life. C earned the money in that period of time.

Numerous valleys merge into this including Val Piumogna that belongs to the Campo Tencia group which is important alpinistically and the Val Bedretto that running along the west coast of the St Gotthard penetrates as far as the high mounts that surround the head of the Val Formazza and ends at the Nufenen Pass. The tundra interspersed with little clumps of arboreal vegetation dominates this region. Pine larch and birch trunks and stumps often come to light in the peat bogs 200 kilometres further north of the present-day taiga. Below us there was a plateau of snow stretching out above us a pale sky empty of snow. Clear proof that the forest has retreated further south. They still held on to the southward without any very great impediments. We reached the peak after two hours. She raised her wrists with her fingers tensed so they would dry. C said she understood.

It looks like a very complicated story but with a little patience you manage to unravel the problem. He hadn't realised how far you could go. While waiting it is suggested you do not stand in the gusts of wind that are quite frequent in this area. The red vehicle had passed yet again without stopping. C moved her arm in his direction. He closes his eyes then opens them again in order to look in a different direction. Moving in more than one direction at the same time. They had warned him it wouldn't be a walk in the park. A sudden rage washed through him hearing her footsteps moving away. Don't be angry with me she said in a whisper. She would always repeat the same thing to me. He spent the night trying to remember her every word. Words are empty they do not have a real existence and so they can be used to fabricate reality. There is nothing else to drink.

On his return he found the house full of strangers. It's obvious we're dealing with a different situation here. There was a wave of laughter in the room. A man rose to get the attention of the entire room. C rose to answer. I tried in vain to stop her before it was too late. What she said didn't totally convince them but it made them admire her for her honesty. I couldn't wait for them to leave. I wanted us to have a few days and nights to be together on our own. She had stopped thinking about the problems that were tormenting her. Perhaps I should kiss her again. When your feelings can't be expressed. He thought he might be able to live without her. In studying a problem we must shun subjectivity one-sidedness and superficiality. The next day a pale sun was illuminating the snowclad landscape. The shells in the drawer had vanished.

Nothing particularly significant had happened. They had met the previous year at C's house. Time had flown past. It was a long story that she didn't feel like telling. After the separation the relationships remained strained. She took away all the things that belonged to her. The next day he telephoned C to find out what his reaction was. C had just fallen asleep when the telephone rang repeatedly. He was worried not seeing her arrive. He had searched for her everywhere. He scrapped the idea of joining C. She had not expected him to come back so quickly. She went to the door and opened it but there was no one there. C stood there for a moment and listened for the sound of a telephone or footsteps. She leant out one last time to see him disappear down the street. Without ever looking back. A big lorry came round the corner. She managed to avoid being run over just in time.

Her straight red hair came to her shoulders. A very light pistachio-coloured dress covering her arms and part of her neck and hugging her hips. Fifth symptom the lack of affection so ignore the emotional storms and the upheaval of passion. I often got him to lend me money. I was broke once and I went to see her. You had mentioned another person who gave you money. No one else gave you any money in that period of time. And what did he do with your money. The women sometimes stayed, for the night. Sometimes. What were they doing with him. That which happens when a woman goes out with a man. Last symptom the characteristic sexual handicaps. One day they went to C together and when the other guests left C told her that she would have to stay with him. At the beginning of our story C was living in C.

The matter in hand obliges me to focus mainly on the concluding events. I'll have to proceed only with references and reminders that knowing the texts can be integrated. Lowering his eyelids he flicked through a few pages. His moving hands touched the silk of the duvet. He confusedly thought that the blanket had been in the other room since the morning. He had a voice of level pitch monotone and relaxing. The fingers immersed. With both nostrils closed and focusing on the tip of your nose hold your breath for as long as you can. She got undressed and went to bed still thinking about those words but being unable to give them any meaning. He was still talking when C fell asleep. On awakening a few hours later he saw C in the same position. He closed his eyes so as not to think. When C woke up he saw that none of them had noticed the book.

She speaks in a slightly infantile voice when she talks about C. And finally the sexual handicap. She has a black dress that goes up to her neck. They spend long hours in the sago swamp from where they emerge with eyes bloodshot from fatigue tired and incapable of any sort of activity. The street is completely deserted and all the windows are closed. Cold hands arid lips. How long does it last. The women grit their teeth to bear the heavy loads they carry on their heads. The loads are usually carried by women because it is said that they have stronger heads. The women's hands like those of the men lie still after the long daily climbs. A raised open hand as if to stop the person you are addressing. The open hand as if to stop the person you want to call. Looking around without seeing him.

C appears at the window. The two indices flank each other rapidly and remain stuck together for a moment. The index finger remains still in front of her mouth as if to keep it shut. The right hand pretends to write on the left hand or vice versa. His right index finger traces an imaginary text printed on his left hand as if it were a page. C is behind the window on the left at the end and she looks around. From the position of her intertwined fingers we can understand what the people in the place we are talking about were like in that moment. C reached out to her she moved away so she would not be touched. Equal and symmetrically opposite hands. Under her hands shapes develop which considered from a tactical point of view take us almost to the limits of intelligibility as all the constructions that are familiar to us and that are above all fixed in us as optical shapes cannot be made unless by accident and as it were through a struggle with oscillation.

He told me about it. Now and again he would tell me you didn't have a penny. And I would say. And he said when you would leave. She always said she preferred not to make too many plans. The third name is not complete. He telephoned over and over again and invited her. Third symptom sincerity. Stronger than the instinct of self-preservation it led him to describe the events with a ferocity not inferior to that which he showed during the events. I don't want to name names but in that period didn't you have relationships with other men. A man gets up and says excuse me. And did you have intimate relations with him. Only once. And then you met C. Yes. Did you have intimate relations with him. Yes. C carries on answering in a subdued tone. Yes. A woman's voice answered me. And did you have intimate relations with C. No. The fourth symptom lucidity is always shown even during the visit and that is typical in the initial phase of the disease.

Some remains of forage were found on the tongue between the molars in the animal's stomach. The botanists of the Petersburg Academy of Science managed to identify a certain number of vegetables amongst these remains. They are the same that are still growing today in the same region. Creeping thyme Thymus serpyllum the horned poppy of the Alps Papaver alpinum var. achantopetala the bitter Nordic buttercup Ranunculus acer borealis there are still a few examples of Thalictrum alpinum the Atragene alpina var. sibirica in the Alps. All the chests are empty. Please note the absence of conifers. The woman answered no certainly not. Two new names were given and a third is easily recognisable. I'd really like to sleep said C. I sleep C replied. C sat on the edge of the bed. A thought suddenly strikes me. It's not cold anymore. So what does it matter. He drew back the sheets. She got up opened the door.

He asked her out he took her to C he had intimate relations with her and he even proposed to her. He told her that they would go away soon and they would never leave each other again. Stroke my hair. Stamp your feet. She touched his face. There were some flowers in a vase and a long sofa in front of the fireplace. In her bright blue eyes. Taking one of her arms. When she heard the lock of the door connecting the two rooms click she reopened her eyes. Both had relations with the two girls. Of course if I had married him he wouldn't have got angry about certain things. What wouldn't he have got angry about. If I had intimate relations with other men. When you married him had you already had intimate relations with C. I don't know. Then that story of their unambiguous simple straightforward relationship. I can't remember anything about what you said to me. All I remember is having been scared one day when I met him on the stairs.

Chapter Eight

The determination of the heat liberated coincided by approximately less than 1 per cent with the values that he had calculated in advance based on the oxygen and carbon dioxide measurements. She sat quite still she was so quiet I wondered if she would faint. C rubbed his neck. She filled the sink and started to scrub herself with the water and a rough towel first the hand that had been splattered with C's blood and then the shoulder she had used to hold the head down. He felt her hand on his shoulders. She was the only person who would comfort me showing me love consideration affection. She kept on thinking about him while C walked up and down the room. They said nothing else to each other. There 's no need for explanations. I think all you need is a little bit of imagination. And now let's not talk about your husband anymore. You know I always think about you. Yes it's very sad. And I spent the afternoon.

I was at C's I slept with him. Yes answered C with an almost imperceptible shrug. One of the wardrobe doors was open and C noticed that there were fewer women's clothes hanging there than the other time. We can also conclude that it must have died in the autumn. Pulling himself up just as he is about to fall off the chair. Stronger than the instinct of self-preservation it led him to describe the events with a ferocity not inferior to that which he showed during the events. They weren't even the same. The sea was calm and flat and the sun was rising. He started running under the sun that was already high in the sky up to where the beach finished. There the rocky walls are so polished and smooth as if a glacier had passed over them. The last class consists of fleeting indices of a movement. This unwanted phenomenon can be contrasted with very shiny paper. It's all written. There was nothing else.

{87}

Can I say something. Do tell. He told C what had happened the other day. I started laughing while I was talking and it worked. We used to see each other almost every day. Then she suddenly changed her attitude. Will you stop laughing. He always wanted something else. She wanted to be on her own. Two people who were too different perhaps. Will you stop interrupting me all the time. Who attract each other with their minds to physically run away like crazy finding themselves close now perhaps only contiguous now. I won't say another word then. C was becoming more and more impatient. The only thing I need is to manage to have a little bit of quiet at last he said. I want to get out of here finally. That said he left the room slamming the door behind him. Doors that open and close letting in air and extracting it through sudden breaks barriers gaps and outlets. All those who had preceded him had got out in rather poor health.

What's so funny. Tomorrow is Saturday no tomorrow is Friday. I helped her to bed and we went to sleep side by side. It always happens like that. Reappearance of traditional weaknesses and old historical legacies under intellectual and moral bodies that had not been capable of fostering a real historical consciousness. This term fills me with horror. He had read a lot of books on the subject since he had become aware of C's failure but this was the only thing that had provided him with an explanation. Nausea or butterflies in your stomach. Walls and ceilings sag slightly in every direction. Of course it could even be a windswept landscape because there are some things that could be trees that have been bent by the wind. She looked out of the window bending forward and stayed in that position for a few minutes. Again no one spoke for a minute or two.

I'd like you to be more with it. Because this sentence by C had a role in the destiny of his life. He stared at the far-off lake and he thought he saw a boat that was heading toward the opposite shore. The sky was completely blue without a cloud and the sun was starting to blaze. C told me that she had had a strange presentiment. C said that he felt like going out going all the way down to the lake to see the boats go by. It was often difficult for her to understand if they were moving normally. They can follow a spatial trajectory while usually only temporal trajectories can be followed. When they arrived near the shore he realised that it must be a very large lake. The coast hides numerous creeks and ravines many of which can only be reached by boat. The wooded point across the bay and further over there the open lake. I saw everything. Then the whole scene disappears.

It is necessary to see other pictures. Secondly it is necessary to have a reasonably precise idea of the writing system used. All those fake sentences that don't mean anything. Literally created from nothing. He thought he heard a sound from the other side of the door but was distracted by his own image reflected in the wardrobe mirror. I am the book. Where the secretions and sedimentations of a by now obsolete and abandoned daily life are accumulated horizontally without any hierarchical order. One thing transforms into another by means of a leap. Signs that are surprised and cut by the vital system of the current communication. Only individual parts but not the whole. I don't know what that means. C turned round completely naked. Where are the things. There's nothing else in the mirror. The completely empty wardrobe. There would be many other things to add but it's not worth it.

I decided to drop in to see her without telling her. She headed off walking quickly between the trees without looking back. Running along the windswept beach. The stretch of coast opposite is very pleasant for both the vistas it offers and the charm of the cliffs below which can be reached via many paths. Bathers in their costumes were sunbathing on the grass. The foghorns of the trawlers off the coast. She went up the stairs. C opened the door after having looked through the peephole. She had fallen asleep on the settee when they rang. C put his arms round her waist and pulled her close. They hug it's not a very comfortable position but they stay together and he strokes her hair. They lay in each other's arms for a long time without talking. He had been waiting for that moment for too long. He stayed until evening C seemed happy. He got up took his jacket and put it on. What's there to eat. C could hardly hear him.

Autism that is the conviction of being a superman who is not subject to the laws of society. C continued talking while I was busy examining the page. C's reflection appears in the mirror. There is no other way of doing it unless you want to stay in the initial situation. It's not easy. If anything black is easier. What do you know about it. If a vessel be suffered to scud before the wind in a very heavy sea much damage is usually done by the shipping of water over her stern and sometimes by the violent plunges she makes forward. Twenty minutes later we climbed on board. At six o'clock in the evening we had regained the beach our canoe was moored to the usual place and the C rocked in the water two miles from the shore. Bit more now lift it. Our canoes were beached about twenty yards away. During the rotation C touches the chest for a moment with her hand. Now pull it all off. They all exist simultaneously. It will never happen again.

Here she went to the bathroom. In this effect they leave together. Due to this the shooting distance is considerably shorter than the breadth of view. C froze in front of the screen that had gone dark. A strange sense of solitude and aloofness from the whole world took hold of C. Let's suppose everything happens just like it does in reality that my body is a system of sense organs in relation with the central organ C. You should lift it up more and open it more with the yellow one. The particles are enlarged by agglutination and they are attached on the walls of the cylinder from which they are taken up by a thin film of water. I grab the glass he hands me and drink slowly. He grabbed it and took another swig. We kept our mouths shut. Only a certain Mr C was talked about but everyone should acknowledge he is one of the main protagonists. It makes me want to laugh.

She continued but she had to stop a little bit further ahead at some traffic lights. The moon which had brightened the first hours of the evening had disappeared. There is a piece about thirty centimetres wide that sticks out both sides of the screen and has some grey stripes placed vertically all along its length. The botanists of the Petrograd Academy of Science managed to identify a certain number of vegetables amongst these remains. The gravel path flanks the new residential holiday village and goes into the woods. In the four canoes which might have been fifty feet long and five broad there were 110 savages in all. C said she understood. Forget everything. Everything takes place in the space between the sheets. Near the end of October he found sleep again, but at the price of terrible dreams. Her hands held his body and she raised her hands to his face and she brushes against it.

In the internal part of the cave along with an abundance of Pleistocene fauna a human Neanderthaloid tooth was recovered. You've already told me this story. The cave is divided into two levels one upper and one lower that host a subterranean lake which can be visited by boat. It might even be another story. They had warned him it wouldn't be a walk in the park. Inside you can go down into a great cavern in the centre of which there is a rock surmounted by a giant stalagmite. We 'll stay and look for another thirty seconds then we 'll leave. All the stories are different one from the other. On returning he found that C had bought herself a new blue silk dress. C remained standing while he explained to her how it had gone. She ran a finger over his lips to wipe the lipstick off them. I have to go. It's still early. I'll be away all day perhaps tomorrow too. He gave her a long kiss on the lips.

First of all one must have a fairly clear idea of the content of the text. But it may no longer be possible after what has happened. The next day a pale sun was illuminating the snow-clad landscape. Further off a cargo ship slowly advances northward on the line of the horizon. Then everything became confusing. Her story weaves and unweaves like the tapestry she was working on. The picture is almost perfectly symmetrical a mirror image. The place where meaning is reduced to surface to signified to appearance and image. A repeated symmetrical arabesque pattern that has no limits to its development and of which no centre exists. It's the unconditional loss of language that starts. He glanced at the piles of clothes on the floor and pushed them to one side. It might never have an end. Should have got up earlier. He decided to leave the same day to understand what had happened.

Sudden postponements of a meeting that is never agreement but a zigzagging path of convulsive truths. I don't think it can go on like this. It depends on the point of view which changes every time C tried to reassure her. I'm sure my destiny is about to change don't you think so too. There's no more time to wait for things to change on their own. She tried to close the door to the veranda. You should try and find out what you really want. If only I could understand who I really am. I just talk nonsense. There is no longer the psychological ego that expresses itself there is no longer the individual that reflects the world through his own single consciousness. That's what is written somewhere. Don't open the door. I don't feel sleepy anymore. C was lying on the bed and was reading. The other possible interpretations are endless but at the moment this is the only reality that belongs to us. She went to the door and opened it but there was no one there.

She suddenly stopped so as not to give away more than she wanted. Since the natural linear characteristics should not appear straight to us over long distances or bisect each other at least one of the ones that are visible in the photograph must be a road. She paused. If the connexion is to be established it can only be through and by means of a third body. You could see a dark blob at the end of the street. The buildings that surround the municipal piazza are the very centre of the town where the traffic is heavy at every hour of the day and night. At the beginning of our story C was living in C. She said that she needed a change of scene. Opening his arms. One of the first sentences that came to his mind. Biting her nails and lips. Still smiling C nodded his head. She had believed once.

{93}

He drank the coffee slowly then put the cup down near the book he was leafing through. His moving hands touched the silk of the duvet. The left hand of which there is only a faint outline seems to thrust into the abdomen. Relax abruptly and rest. Some figures appeared on the screen which were immediately taken down by those present. She looked up and looked fixedly at him. She was the only person who comforted me showing me love consideration affection. C was walking by her side in silence. Going to the left without getting close to the row of poles is dangerous. C had stopped he looked around holding his breath. A few drops of sweat beaded his tanned face. There is a third type of conflict that occurs when one has set off along a familiar path to pursue a certain end and a new and fascinating opportunity presents itself.

She saw some distant lights that were moving on the side of the mountain. Their shape and direction change continuously and sometimes even their colour. She mulled over it for a while then she decided to resume the discussion. He starts talking to her gently. The attempt proved fruitless but a few weeks later they decide to go on a trip. From there they had reached C by plane. Mammoths and reindeer would wander the cold steppes in the rare conifer woods and with them lived bison wild horses hares arctic foxes. They spend long hours in the sago swamp from where they emerge with eyes bloodshot from fatigue tired and incapable of any sort of activity. Three thick cables clearly spaced penetrated into the dock dropping from a pole and supported by two others they went back toward the house on the opposite side of the road. Following the movement of the cables.

Once the construction has been made every movement every suspicious inclination is marvellously compensated by a shift in the centre of gravity of the body. It concerns three different movements not a single continuous movement. When the smoke comes out of the boiler it passes into the cylinder where the solid particles cannot get through this type of hydraulic diaphragm which is one metre thick. He took a few steps then turned toward her. The girl's slender body trembled convulsively. She has a moment of uncertainty. For a moment she stood stock-still then she noticed her whole body was trembling violently. She had the sheet pulled up to her shoulders. Lying on the ground forehead down legs together hands under his body at shoulder height palms on the floor. All wet. C enters wrapped in a blanket. You don't have a temperature anymore.

She looked into his eyes while she was thinking she would never manage to tell him the truth. She told me that we would have to get married sooner or later. C looks at him through the windowpane. From this last series we have chosen the pictures that interested us because they offer a greater probability of discovering signs of life. Because he had total control over my life. Get him to tell you about all the things in my drawers. Then because of the very nature of things we shall in the end witness a raising of consciousness which moreover is very limited. Then he said that that evening he had returned home late had drunk a lot and had gone to sleep. So I left. When I arrived C was already ready and waiting for me. She accompanied him to the door and said goodbye to him on the doorstep. C's clothes were neatly folded on the chair. There are enormous shapes of giant mammoths on the curve of this arch.

She was bursting with joie de vivre while she was chatting with the two girls by her side who were laughing at something she had just said. You are lying on the settee with the telephone on the floor constantly moving. Let it dry for a few minutes then touch up again with the brush and the cosmetic. C sat on the edge of the bed. I sleep C replied. The grey paint on the walls of the corridor smelt fresh there weren't any doors and the light came from the lamps hanging from the ceiling. The events of the last twenty-four hours had been a true test of his intellectual ability and now while it was as if he were paralysed in the moonlight his face reflected a greenish pallor that was not only due to the rays of the moon. Yet he realised he still didn't know anything about her.

She turned toward him. How he had changed. We could have done without that. He looked toward the window where C had been. In the picture of C the breasts have five circular lines the pelvic arch and the stomach six. Of course if I had married him he wouldn't have got angry about certain things. Did the women sometimes stay the night. Sometimes. I couldn't say how old she is exactly. The above-mentioned researchers in repeated experiments carried out on patients who were made to regress to the first month of their lives managed to obtain an extension reflex typical in newborn babies. Despite this restriction the number of details observed was sufficient to draw some conclusions. Let's not stop here. They went on like this for a good half an hour. Some weeks passed and they met in C's house again to discuss the new situation that had been created. To have fun.

Chapter Nine

Why can't I leave my husband said C. I think all you need is a little bit of imagination. In a series of ties that did not seem very binding but had quickly become indispensable the new applications the new career prospects the new consumer goods a better standard of living. We 'll only find out in a few days' time. No tonight is impossible. There 's no point in making a fuss about it. Neorealism was very important for the middle generation. But I don't feel very well. So we love each other. Then C leans against the wall and stays with her back turned. The music stops and she turns to look. C chases her around the flat while they swear at each other. C turns. Well there 's nothing sad about it. She takes a book and C joins her. Staring at her. One month later C telephoned in the dead of night.

I saw a trickle of water dribble out from under the bathroom door. Its rocky walls are so polished and smooth as if a glacier had passed over them. The vaults were composed of compact non-porous limestone which was totally covered with tiny lime crystals from the condensation. There are enormous shapes of giant mammoths on the curve of this arch. I was quiet. I could not add anything here other than my previous observations. He was looking for another story to tell. The fourth symptom lucidity is always shown even during the visit and that is typical in the initial phase of the disease. He looked up at me quickly and looked away again. No trace of human habitation was found inside the caverns.

What are you waiting for. Back and forth. You could at least shut the door. C had had enough of waiting. He was really upset when he found out that C had no intention of coming back. Strange rumours were circulating. Each on its own. We tried he thought ruefully. Ciao. That said he left the room slamming the door behind him. A barge would pass at times. He didn't even pretend to dry them off. There the river looks like a rivulet and the trees go down all the way to the bank. The water is green and glassy especially on the other side. Tears were rolling down his face. I don't really know where this is going. Nothing ever happens anyway. He stared blankly at the flowing water. All useless words. There was something he wanted to tell me and he did not know where to begin. There are some pages missing here. Stop asking all those questions. Looks like it's trying to rain. The red eyes. Sitting on the ground. Time heals all wounds.

It looks like it might be a seaside scene even though the jetty has gone and it gives the impression of a stretch of land emerging out of the water that is rough and reflects a little sunlight and the sunlight filters through the clouds. I've skipped a passage. What's so funny. In your condition. How long does it last. He was groping his way across the room toward the light switch. He squinted slightly. From the open door I see the meadow that slowly turns light blue and then silvery. How did you get this scar I asked. C switched the light off muttering to himself. He was not all that interested in what she was saying. She had a thin white line on her stomach. He reached into the darkness for the bottle. Moving his hand slowly. I'm willing to do anything to help him. As he walked by the bed he trod on something that was warm squelchy and smooth.

It seemed to C that all hope was lost. He opened another bottle and filled his glass. It has been programmed in such a way that it can never ever deprogramme itself. He wondered whether his life really had any meaning. He stared at the far-off lake and he thought he saw a boat that was heading toward the opposite shore. It was built so that each part was independent but at the same time could be linked to the others. At least he hoped so. C had told him once that if he went on in this vein he would run the risk of being misunderstood. What do I care he said that's not the problem. He had given up smoking. She was walking up and down the beach. C was wearing a light dress that came just above the knee. One must be open to the thing that is being born that is shapeless magmatic it seems like it resembles life. He saw her stop for a second to pick something up from the sand.

Trying to escape was useless. So I jumped into the car closed the door I leant out of the window and burst out laughing. There is no longer the psychological ego that expresses itself there is no longer the individual that reflects the world through his own single consciousness. I turned the car and pulled up. Which way now. I haven't got a clue. I can't bear it any longer. Give me the money. Retching. The end of the cycle. And that's how this story ends. Even though you can always start again from scratch. In the verbal landscape. Where the secretions and sedimentations of a by now obsolete and abandoned daily life are accumulated horizontally without any hierarchical order. She was not listening to him anymore. A horizontal association that unleashes fresh vitality that revives the dead. C had wandered off evidently bored by the turn of events.

To be used when the subject is in shadow or backlit that is when the light source is behind the subject. He downed his drink and while the waiter was bringing him another he looked at me with anxious eyes as if I were the only friend he had left. Bathers in their costumes were sunbathing on the grass. I saw a flash of hope in his eyes. Everything was close palpitating in the strong light. He wondered whether C really missed him and had a moment of angst. The programme cannot be stopped or modified once it has been started. Other pictures overlap without any specific order some are out of focus and nearly unrecognisable. She grabbed his hand and squeezed it with all her strength. A book fell on the floor and C did not bend down to pick it up. He ardently wanted to kiss her. The sudden roar of a plane in the clear sky made him look up.

This being done we hoisted jib and mainsail kept full and we start boldly out to sea. All directions are of equal importance. She had put the glass on the table within reach but then she had picked it up. They all exist simultaneously. And after an hour we had had enough. She sat down again on the bed. Biting her lower lip. Her hair between her lips. C continued talking while I was busy examining the page. Nothing has been deleted. Maybe. Why not. I mean it. Blood beats in her temples her hands tremble and her eyes glaze over. Her eyes open wide her muscles tense her heart pounds. She wrings her hands nervously blinking rapidly. Don't you feel cold. It will never happen again. I don't want to meet any of the others on the contrary I want to avoid them.

Every now and then she opened her mouth wide and I could see her tongue that was moving slightly. The wind has entirely ceased but it is evident that we are still hurrying on to the south under the influence of a powerful current. We kept our mouths shut. Open your hand. The left hand of which there is only a faint outline seems to thrust into the abdomen. All written down. The arms increase the length of the body and the hands appear to be under the lower limbs. The crudely carved fingers seem to thrust into the abdomen. All interest is accentuated in the harmonious relationship between the curvature of the thighs and that of the abdomen. The navel cavity is accentuated. The fingers immersed. All the rest has been eliminated. After a while she sighed got up and went into the water. C awoke after an hour and went into the bathroom to get some water. He grabbed it and took another swig. Come on let's continue.

He started moving faster. Until he had enough. Well get a move on. First I filled the glasses then I slowly crossed the meadow up to the pink oleanders that were growing on the riverbank. This view shows a rather weak glimmer of light upward with a strip of dark in the centre and an even weaker and more diffuse light toward the lower part. He empties the glass and puts it on the bedside table. From the window. He came out of the bathroom she clenched her fists and got in the shower. C swimming off described an arc then he turned coming back in a straight line toward me and got out of the water. It was not raining. As a result of the abundant wealth of phyto and zooplankton also aided by the slimy riverbed there live numerous species of fish some of which are native others have been introduced to the waters including the lake whitefish the char the pike the shad the carp the tench the bleak the European chub the eel and the trout which are extremely sought after for their excellent meat and may reach a considerable size.

He switched off the light and went to the window and looked outside. He screwed up his eyes looking at the horizon veiled in mist. Red and yellow flowers spring up among the bushes. They are still shooting from the other side of the woods. Making her body lurch forward. Clinging on as best she could. I let myself go I don't usually do that. Words are empty they do not have a real existence and so they can be used to fabricate reality. There 's nothing to laugh about. We arrived in C at the dead of night. The town was shrouded in fog. There wasn't a soul in sight. You've already told me this story. C suddenly changed her attitude and went back to lie down on the bed. The scar on her stomach was visible in the faint dusk light. You could actually close the window. Words like objects. She flicked her hand as if she were trying to shoo something away. Then the telephone started ringing again.

His dreams became more and more distressing. Dead bodies strewn in the rubble. The glow of the fires in the darkness of the night and the flashes of the explosions the plumes of smoke. Then everything became confusing. Dense dark smoke was enveloping everything. Silence was falling. All you could hear was the sound of the water rushing past. She got out of the bath and stared at him hesitantly. It could have been the last time. I'd like to say something. Leave me alone. Before it all ends. It is the moment in which you realise that language offers no guarantee at all. There is no meaning but something like a dream of meaning. C moved away from the window with an annoyed look on her face. They let the telephone ring and ring without answering it. He grabbed her by the arm. They had nothing else to say to each other. There is nothing else to drink. He thought he might be able to live without her.

You could hear the sound of the sea and the breaking of the waves. I don't know where this is going. After all that's happened. There are pages and pages that closely deal with the issues we are interested in. He shifted his weight onto his left leg. He placed his foot on the window ledge. I don't think it can go on like this. He could not see anything so he turned toward the door at the end of the corridor. C stood there for a moment and listened for the sound of a telephone or footsteps. He tried the door handle but it was locked. They are not suitable things for any old reader. Besides there is nothing to understand. His lips were quivering slightly. C raced in waving his arms and shouting something that she did not catch. A thousand ideas came into his head all at the same time. They went back into the corridor and locked the door. He did not manage to read to the end. I'd like something to drink.

Clench your teeth and fists. A very light pistachio-coloured dress covering her arms and part of her neck and hugging her hips. To his left a woman nearly doubled over her neck really extended a flat nose a pronounced bosom her hands outstretched toward the man. In the picture of C the breasts have five circular lines the pelvic arch and the stomach six. Then she lifts her feet and lets herself sink. There were some flowers in a vase and a long sofa in front of the fireplace. My husband came toward me I was scared he was going to beat me I covered my face with my hands. Then he got into his car parked by the kerb a white car. At the end of the narrow street the traffic lights are stuck on red. He was wearing a blue coat he got into the car and left.

The boat was going through the water at a terrific rate full before the sail no reef in either jib or mainsail running her bows completely under the foam. Cut to the chase. I'm going to carry on. Go on. Well it looks stupendous. And I was wondering how he had the audacity to talk about the Resistance and not feel sick when talking about the present. He looked for his glass and took another draught. I grab the glass he hands me and drink slowly. His head was heavy and he could feel that his lips nostrils and eyelids were puffy. Lowering his eyelids he flicked through a few pages. He stops to look at him fascinated. Why don't you look at me. Why don't you come down. Why do you ask. Everything was moving. I looked over toward the bed. From that moment the political reaction started that should have brought into question the institutional battle itself.

She speaks in a slightly infantile voice when she talks about C. I had already noticed it but it appeared more evident on her tanned skin now. Because I love my husband. She said she had gone for a walk along the shore of the lake. And you used to go to bed with other men while you were living with him. Yes with C. Her thighs were two parallel lines which then terminated. The legs are simply formed by straight lines with pointed tips. Their shape and direction change continuously and sometimes even their colour. I helped her to bed and we went to sleep side by side. He took her face in his hands and kissed her. And finally the sexual handicap. Walls and ceilings sag slightly in every direction. Following the movement of the cables. I had never told her that during our last meeting C had repeatedly claimed he still loved her.

{106}

There 's nothing else to drink. She was wearing a beige linen dress with a red scarf. C is wearing a tweed jacket with leather elbow patches a light jumper and grey trousers. His right index finger traces an imaginary text printed on his left hand as if it were a page. She was wearing a long black wool skirt that reached her toes. I'm really drunk. Not so fast. There 's no more coffee. You don't have a temperature anymore. Mummy's boy's downstairs. While the ship was stopping. All wet. Sudden darkness and get that thingy down here. One leg was extended and spread and you feel C's fingers in your hair. It is clear that the horizon is completely dark and you can just make it out vaguely. He then went into the room switched on the lights and looked around. C reached out to her but she moved away so she would not be touched. He looked at his hands.

He had remained in silence the whole journey. The cavity ends on the left in a low arch in the rock inside which a funnel-shaped alcove penetrates into the darkness. He came down into the lobby using the stairs. Bronchial diseases and pulmonary emphysemas increase in a short time. Not too distant from C's great hall with its central pillar of rock there is a shallow chamber where stands a large wall that is more than twenty metres wide. She goes into the bathroom finding a warmer environment there and lets the boiling water run into the bath. The cold water that was touching his body and ruffling his hair made him shiver. After periods of eruptions drops of hard calcareous water from the mountain streams filter down through the rocks and gradually leave transparent strata on the walls or form columns of stalactites or stalagmites that hang from the vault or rise from the floor until they meet.

He walked on the grass between the trees. Pine larch and birch trunks and stumps often come to light in the peat bogs 200 km further north of the present-day taiga. His face is very pale he does not seem adequately nourished for such an unspeakable expenditure of energy. He looked her in the face. It doesn't matter. Why should I hate. Everything takes place in the space between the sheets. The lake and the road could be seen from there. So what does it matter. He drew back the sheets. Now that's better. She was clutching her hands to her chest careless of her newly-polished nails. At a certain point. What do I care. There is no irony in it. Near the end of October he found sleep again but at the price of terrible dreams.

All imaginable pathways of the line that represents a direct connexion to the objective are equally impracticable and no adjustment of the shape of the body to the spatial forms of the surrounding objects can allow the objective to be reached. She spins round in a fit of rage. She was exhausted. She was furious and a wave of rage rose from her neck to her ears. The whole body vibrates the head clearly stands out the arched back extends from its extremity and the tension of the arms drawn diagonally continues from the line of the back. Then trams buses and private vehicles started to stop repeatedly from the outskirts toward the centre in Piazzale del Cimitero Monumentale in Foro Buonaparte in Piazza Fontana along Cerchia dei Navigli. We could have done without that. From start to finish. Let's not stop here. Then you start again. Tremors perspiration weight loss and exophthalmia soon followed. All around the landscape was immersed in darkness.

Chapter Ten

Despite the contrast of the negative which might be natural the result is usable. Neorealism was very important for the middle generation. There 's no point in making a fuss about it. And him what did he say. But things have changed they have gone in a different direction while we were chatting about all our nice little plans. The generation of social commitment. Oh I'm not all that sad. And now let's not talk about your husband anymore. Here you have the clear impression of a sky at sunset or sunrise with the sun that is shining through the clouds producing a sort of diffuse brightness. Hence we can acknowledge that a perfect similarity of colour with a certain background does not on its own constitute camouflage at all. At sunset the horizon to the north is clear. Fishing in the lake. Looking at him fixedly. Because I can't leave my husband C said.

She fights it by continually creating new verbal situations. Can I proceed with my project. This implies the movement of the head the torsion of the torso a general contraction and an acceleration of the pulse and respiration. Changing the subject for the first time. He stopped telephoning and for all the rest of the evening he subjected me to an absurd interrogation. I don't want to name names but in that period didn't you have relationships with other men. Yes answered C with an almost imperceptible shrug. And then. Now and again he would tell me you didn't have a penny. If you don't mind the question. Ask me something else if you want. At six C came down to the bar and ordered a vodka with tonic water and a slice of lemon. Pointing to a guy who was sitting wrapped up in an overcoat. A man gets up and says excuse me. We reached the hotel by taxi at about eleven o'clock.

He felt a strange emotion wash over him. A sort of nihilism for which he felt a profound fondness. The man in the street can get out of his responsibilities by simply claiming that the matter does not concern him. If you keep going down this road you'll definitely lose me. On the way he thought back to that afternoon on the seashore. Do you see what I want from you. There was something he wanted to tell me and he did not know where to begin. We can understand each other she said knowingly. C was behaving as if nothing had happened. C would always say that there was time to die. He had felt better after having thrown up. The only thing I need is to manage to have a little bit of quiet at last. While they go back to the hotel the sun has just set. Villages of red-tile-roofed houses perch atop hills or cling precariously to the mountainsides.

I'm afraid it's a bit like this for everyone. A few seconds later we were on the beach. He had walked for hours and hours before reaching the river. You take the not very appealing path but after about a hundred metres the road improves and you can continue without any problems along the noisy foamy river thick with willows. Every now and then you can hear voices coming from the rear of the villa. Scathing sarcastic unkind retorts. He came back into the room and headed toward the window. She saw some distant lights that were moving on the side of the mountain. C could never manage to get up at a decent hour in the morning and didn't have the slightest idea of the value of money. Which you could enjoy more fully if you did not spend hours and hours on the phone but got out and looked for more real relationships.

The sentences not only undergo the normal deprivation of their intrinsic value and communication capacity but acquire acceleration and a centripetal and centrifugal force at the same time. It's obvious that the story couldn't go on like this. It's all just a story of sentences. That time she followed him without making too much of a fuss. The last time they had met had been one week earlier on the beach. Everyone knew about their story by now. C told me that she had had a strange presentiment. I answered that things would probably change. I'll do my best he answered with mild embarrassment. Her skin was warm and moist. What do I care he said that's not the problem. Okay okay I get it. He watched her head toward the bathroom naked picking up her handbag from the bedside table. She dialled the number while the water was running. A halfasleep voice answered.

Secondly it is necessary to have a reasonably precise idea of the writing system used. The road winds along mountainous slopes and every now and then spectacular gorges suddenly appear behind the hairpin bends. In the verbal landscape. Stalagmites and stalactites meet in a fantastic setting where mirages of rocks are lavishly reflected in the clear waters of the subterranean basins. Soon after that C came out of the bathroom covering himself with a yellow towel. I tried to get her to understand that she really had to change her life. The light is that soft light we have in May without shadows. Otherwise all that would become impossible. Money wasn't an issue. C didn't know how to answer and only told half-truths. Her body tightens. Beads of sweat form on the back of his neck armpits forehead and cheeks. Then she had raced off to lock herself in the bathroom. A long time had gone by.

{113}

No new ideas coming from the young. Sometimes the past pulls harder on you than the future. Our generation however preferred dealing with practical things. He carried on talking to hold her attention. He described his project in minute detail. The remaining part of the field including the long sides has a decoration similar to that of the central rectangle. He could not find another solution. The red cylinder that rotates extremely rapidly. The shade of the tree that was covering them. Pulling her gently to himself. Everything was close palpitating in the strong light. The foghorns of the trawlers off the coast. The stretch of coast opposite is very pleasant for both the vistas it offers and the charm of the cliffs below which can be reached via many paths. He had hung all his hopes on that meeting. He stopped talking worried he would bore her.

She invited them home for a coffee then they went out with C. They meet in a restaurant she smiles at him first. I went straight over to C because I wanted to talk to her. C told him about the meeting she had had that morning. He gave other names. And after an hour we had had enough. This being done we hoisted jib and mainsail kept full and we start boldly out to sea. Twenty minutes later we climbed on board. Vomiting over the side leaning on the ropes. Dark blue of the panorama. Ten seconds. But it could end at any time whenever you want. The moment a shift occurs the white becomes dominant and the black background and so on for every subsequent change. It should be number 47 now. There is no other way of doing it unless you want to stay in the initial situation.

She chose a patch of shade under the branches of the tree next to C and stretched out calmly on the dry grass that pricked her skin through her light dress. She got undressed and went to bed still thinking about those words but being unable to give them any meaning. In the darkness the screen emitted a pale light you could hear the soft swishing of the sea in the distance. The navel cavity is accentuated. You come down with this thing the mammoth. From the study of the seeds found we can conclude that it must have died in the autumn. Zero blue where 's the mammoth under the skyscrapers. C froze in front of the screen that had gone dark. The road ran high cut into the heart. The boat was going through the water at a terrific rate full before the sail no reef in either jib or mainsail running her bows completely under the foam.

The minutes were ticking away slowly. The same impression as before with the brighter light from above and the area of light in the background that extends toward the edge becoming almost a strip of light along the lower side. Now that's better. He looked her in the face. He said it didn't matter. He has a considerable ability to attract attention and influence others although they distrust him a little. I suddenly felt concerned for C and I breathed a sigh of relief when I saw her again. C swimming off described an arc then he turned coming back in a straight line toward me and got out of the water. I went back up on the bridge being careful not to slip on the oily iron ladder. The device is based on ultrasound and is composed of a metallic cylinder at one end of which is placed a whistle generator of ultrasounds that are reflected to the other end of the cylinder with an adjustable cap.

{115}

The day passed uneventfully after the trip to the cave and lunch by the seaside. It looks like a very complicated story but with a little patience you manage to unravel the problem. In the film he 's dying under a tree and she walks off. The question is not so much the story itself but rather what effects it might produce what developments it might have what dynamics it might set in motion. The perpetual mobility of a desire of a dream without time or space. The combinations are endless. All the stories are different one from the other. It's all like a game. It had all started that morning on the beach. At the restaurant C had managed to make her see that she should not feel tied down because of what had happened. I don't know what happened to me. I let myself go I don't usually do that. You could even start from another episode and obtain a slightly different story. Though the question is rather irrelevant.

In studying a problem we must shun subjectivity one-sidedness and superficiality. Where should you start. First of all one must have a fairly clear idea of the content of the text. C got out of the bath and stared at him hesitantly. And finally an element that may suggest a starting hypothesis is needed. She remembered the first time they had gone to C. There are vistas of olive groves vineyards lush valleys and mountain peaks at every turn. You can see rosettes rosebuds lozenges and other plant and flower forms laid out according to a rigid scheme. C now appeared to be in a very good mood. Between the triangular spires and the alcoves of the central rectangle there is on both sides a flowering bush with little birds that are also stylised. C had slept nearly the whole journey. All this does not have very much to do with our story but it doesn't matter.

{116}

Nothing particularly significant had happened. C got into the car and said let's go I'm in a hurry. It had been anticipated that this would happen. Occasions like this will probably never happen again he thought. He lit a cigarette and threw the match out of the car window. I have to go said C it's going to be a tough day tomorrow. There is no obligation to finish a sentence it is infinitely catalysable one may always add something. And so until the end of our lives. That's what is written somewhere. It's a book that made me understand the mysteries of life. He did not manage to read to the end. Once the green line was crossed I turned left to get to the seafront. It runs along the whole city for approximately three kilometres and is very popular with the inhabitants and tourists during the day and in the evening who love wandering round the countless vendors' stalls enjoying the salty smell.

He was wearing a blue coat he got into the car and left. If you continue to drive very fast you can even complete the trip in two and a half days but it is more sensible to give yourself three. He couldn't see anything else because a veil of cloud had covered the whole landscape. There is a dark line in the water that could be a dock or a breakwater or something like that. Nevertheless we are almost certainly talking about a natural peninsula. He was walking carefully as if the paving hurt his feet. To this end the research carried out by Gildo Frank Bowers Buch True and Stephenson on the plantar reflex of the big toe is particularly interesting. You could see a dark blob at the end of the street. He went on until he could hear the sound of water beneath him. To his left a woman nearly doubled over her body really extended a flat nose a pronounced bosom her hands outstretched toward the man.

After having run along the east bank of the lake the road crosses a deep crack at the bottom of which the turbulent waters flow. All right then let's do this. I was only ten years old when the war ended and so I didn't realise that the war had finished and so I missed the great experience of the Liberation. He didn't earn any money in that period of time. The problem of the maximal shooting distances must again be remembered. Everything has been thoroughly studied and all obstacles foreseen. I don't really fancy it that much. Let them write in the meantime. Yeah but I don't know how they do it. Keep your leg raised for fifteen seconds then relax. She wanted to have a swim but decided it would be better to telephone C straight away. He drank the coffee slowly then put the cup down near the book he was leafing through. When C woke up he saw that none of them had noticed the book.

The attempt proved fruitless but a few weeks later they decide to go on a trip. They had left their room toward evening and had departed by train for C. They didn't get in touch with anyone for several weeks. They spent most of their time shut up in the room sleeping reading or talking. Today tomorrow or never. She smiled at him knowingly then picked up the receiver and dialled a number. She has a black dress that goes up to her neck. She had a thin white line on her stomach. His clothes did not survive but the way the numerous mammoth-tusk ornaments are laid out allows us to reconstruct the shape of the waistcoat and trousers. The legs are simply formed by straight lines with pointed tips. The lines reach up as far as the tip of the pole and there they stop abruptly. It wasn't there before. A pole without roots planted in the ground and not even being planted deep enough.

As all the constructions that are familiar to us and that are above all fixed in us as optical shapes cannot be made unless by accident and as it were through a struggle with oscillation. She would wear a vibrant red velvet dress with a gold belt and the wide erminelined sleeve would show a glimpse of her bare arm as it rested on the banister behind her. She has a moment of uncertainty. C passes behind the window. She turns to the window stroking her hair. She was rather tidy and seemed much tidier than she actually was until you looked at her white face with her wan lips and without lipstick impassive and smooth a curiously cold and rigid smoothness. In the end he fell back onto the pillows. Change scenes the hippo disappears. You'd told me it was a long story.

C's clothes were neatly folded on a chair. She listened to what he was saying as she was going in and out of the bathroom. Every phrase was repeated twice at a distance of time. I'll show you a detailed plan at the appropriate moment. The chamber ends on the left in a low arch in the rock against which a funnel-shaped alcove penetrates into the darkness. Besides the rivers rarely flow parallel to a coast or parallel to each other for any distance roads however often follow the coast and it is not infrequent that they run parallel to each other. No trace of human habitation was found inside the caverns. Racing down the steps of a metro station. The mortality of the elderly reaches very high peaks. The situation was becoming particularly serious in Piazzale XXIV Maggio and at Porta Ticinese.

He looked her in the face. He went back into the room and closed the door. Well what does it matter. They are the same that are still growing today in the same region. Some remains of forage were found on the tongue between the molars in the animal's stomach. The grey paint on the walls of the corridor smelt fresh there weren't any doors and the light came from the lamps hanging from the ceiling. C opened the other door to the bathroom softly and entered a room that was exactly the same as hers. But there was nothing to see. Where have you been. I'd really like to sleep said C. The moon which had brightened the first hours of the evening had disappeared. Yet he realised he still didn't know anything about her. Finally satisfied with the changes made to the scene he returned to the armchair he had chosen and made himself comfortable with his right foot dangling over the armrest.

Now C had turned round sweetly so that he was boxed in between her and the rail. She gives him a long kiss stroking his hair. No other sound except that of the water falling on their two entwined bodies. C told her they had to come back. Turning round and looking at him in the face. She knew she would finally leave him for C sooner or later and this was the whole story. A word like any other. I couldn't say how old she is exactly. I think he wants to talk to you about C. When you married him had you already had intimate relations with C. It was a long time before I met you. What were they doing with him. You had mentioned another person who gave you money. All she had to say. I don't have any more money. It's useless for defending yourself or fighting against anything.

THE UNIVERSITY OF
WINCHESTER